FIRST
AMONG
THE
DEAD

A CONSTABLE TYLER NEISH NOVELLA

ZERT⬡X
CRIME

CHAPTER
ONE

CONSTABLE TYLER NEISH had never seen a dead body before. Not like this. Not up close.

Sure, he'd seen photos. Everyone had seen photos. Dismembered murder victims, headless corpses in road traffic accidents, an old man who'd tried crossing a frozen canal without success.

These had all been presented to him during his training. He'd nodded along with the rest of the recruits, and tried his best not to throw up in his mouth.

Especially at the headless one.

But photographs were one thing. Seeing an actual dead person in the flesh was something entirely different.

He lay just off to the left of the path, face down, half-covered by snow. One arm was stretched ahead of him, like he'd been trying to crawl into the house just a few yards further up the path.

His hand was purple, like a bruise, the skin raw where the cold had been nipping away at it all night.

There were no other footprints in the snow beyond those of the man himself. No streaks of blood on the covering of white to mark this as anything other than a tragic accident.

Tyler had already pieced the story together based on what he could see and what he'd been told. A man in his forties, out on a Christmas night out, too pissed and too cold to make it all the way back to the warmth and safety of his house.

He'd either fallen or decided in his drunken fug to have himself a wee lie down on the grass, where he'd likely fallen asleep and succumbed to the sub-zero temperatures.

And now, here he was. Just lying there. The first actual dead body Tyler had seen in his nearly twenty-one years on Earth.

He'd been both dreading this moment and hoping for it. Well, no, not 'hoping.' That sounded terrible. He didn't mean it like that.

But you couldn't be a proper copper until you'd stared death in the face. It wasn't the training or the uniform that moulded a civilian into a police officer, it was the experience.

It was this. Now. That first dead body. That was how you earned your place.

You could prepare for it with photos, and first-hand accounts, and video footage all you liked, but none of that was the same. None of that could ready you for the real thing.

Tyler thumbed the radio on his shoulder and called it in. The ambulance would come. Scene of Crime, too, maybe, just in case. He was too new to the job for them to trust his opinion on anything, so they'd want to check it out. Probably just as well.

Turning, he cast his eye across the houses over the road, just in time to see their window coverings twitching. It was still early—his first shout of the day—and lights burned behind the curtains and through gaps in the blinds. He saw himself reflected in a few of the glass panes. Even from this distance, his uniform looked two sizes too big. Right then, it felt that way, too.

He stamped his feet and rubbed some warmth into his hands. His breath formed a cloud as he whispered a, 'Right, then,' before approaching the body again, the snow crunching beneath his shoes. He hadn't checked for a pulse, he realised. He was supposed to do that first. That was basic common sense.

Squatting, he pressed a finger against the man's throat. Nothing. Not a flicker. Not a thump. Mind you, his hands were so cold that the pulse could've been going like a jackhammer, and he likely wouldn't have felt anything.

Tyler lowered his head and took a moment to pay his respects. Around him, the street was silent and still, as if it, too, was mourning the loss.

It was a sad, stupid, pointless death. A life tragically snuffed out like a—

'Waaargh!'

The man on the ground reared up like he'd been struck by lightning, coughing and wheezing and spluttering out clumps of wet snow.

'Jesus fuck!' Tyler screeched. He launched himself

backwards, like he was trying to get out of the path of a speeding train, then stumbled, fell, and landed arse-first in a puddle of slushy grey snow.

'What's happening?' the man on the ground cried. His face was red, like it had been burned by the cold, and his bloodshot eyes seemed to swivel in different directions as they desperately tried to make sense of his surroundings. 'Where am I? What's happening? The fuck is this?'

An icy shiver shot up Tyler's spine. Partly, it was the shock of the man so forcefully coming back to life, but mostly it was the puddle.

'You're not dead!' he cried, pointing at the man in a way that came across as quite accusatory. 'You're supposed to be dead!'

This didn't do much to ease the other man's panic.

'What are you saying that for?' he gasped, rising onto his knees and patting at himself as if making sure he was still solid. 'Why would you say that? What do you mean I'm meant to be dead? Were you trying to kill me?'

'What? No! You were lying in the snow all night. You weren't moving. I thought you'd died!' Tyler shot back.

Adrenaline had got the man up and bobbing from foot to foot, like he was readying himself for a boxing match, or was desperate for a slash.

'What? Fuck. All night? What do you mean, all night?' he demanded. His bottom jaw began to vibrate, his teeth clattering together as his brain finally registered the cold. 'When are we on? What time is it?'

Tyler glanced down at his watch. 'It's quarter past eight,' he said, hauling himself back up to his feet. Most of the puddle came with him, rivulets of icy water running down the backs of his legs from his soaking wet arse.

'Half eight? What, in the morning?'

'Aye.'

The man responded by ejecting a long, throaty syllable that rose in pitch and volume the longer it went on.

'Fuuuuuuuuuuuuuuuuuuck!'

He hobbled up the path towards the front door, then stopped on the step just long enough to announce, 'This isn't my house!'

With that, he went charging back down the path, shaking his head and glaring at Tyler as he rushed past him.

'Thanks for nothing, pal,' he spat, and then he hurried out of the garden and went lurching off along the street.

Shivering in the cold and the wet, Tyler watched him until he disappeared around the corner at the far end of the street. Only then did he press the button on his shoulder-mounted radio again.

'Eh, this is PC Neish to control,' he said. 'About that ambulance…'

CHAPTER
TWO

'WELL, well, well. If it isn't Zombie Boy.'

Tyler unzipped his high-vis jacket, tutted below his breath, then turned to see which of his fellow new starts had made the joke.

If you could even call it a joke. He wasn't sure it technically qualified. For one thing, it wasn't funny, despite what the polite laughter of half a dozen recently minted police constables might suggest.

For another thing, it didn't make any sense. He wasn't the one who'd come back to life, so why was he the Zombie Boy? There was no logic to the nickname, it was just a low-hanging fruit.

'Your banter's shite,' Tyler said, at which point the room fell silent around him. More than silent, in fact. It was as if the whole briefing room had tipped over into negative sound.

It took him just a few moments to realise why. The person who had made the remark was not, in fact, one of his fellow constables. The nasal whine of the speaker's voice should've been enough of a warning.

Chief Inspector Samuel 'Snecky' Grant had earned his nickname thanks to his thick Invernesian accent. 'Snecky' was a slang term for Inverness itself, and given that his accent was so firmly of the place that it bordered on the cartoonish, he now shared in the label, too.

Snecky had taken it upon himself to act as a guide and mentor to the new starts. He apparently did this every time, but got bored after a week or so. That's what some of the older constables had told the newbies, anyway, but it had already been ten days, and the Chief Inspector was showing no sign of losing interest.

'I'm sorry, Constable Neish?' he said, very deliberately touching a finger to an ear and pushing it forward. 'Did you say something, there?'

Tyler felt all eyes in the room watching him. The six other new starts stood rooted to the spot in terror. The nine or ten older hands who sat on chairs facing the front of the room tried very hard not to laugh.

'I, eh, I said *good one*, boss.' Tyler summoned a smile to try to sell the response, but his heart wasn't in it.

He'd spent most of the day standing on the edge of an industrial estate with a speed gun as the snow piled up on the flat of his cap, and his bum cheeks were yet to thaw out from the morning's misadventures.

Snecky sniffed. 'Yes. Yes, I thought that's probably what you said.' He flicked his gaze up and down, taking in the measure of the young constable. 'And it's *sir*, not *boss*.'

'Yes, boss.' Tyler flinched. 'Sorry, yes, sir.'

A couple of the older constables sniggered, and Tyler felt his cheeks sting red. Then again, it was mid-December in the Highlands of Scotland, so they'd been stinging red for most of the day.

'You will be pleased to know that the reanimated corpse of Mr Wilson made it home safely,' Snecky said, really milking the whole thing for all it was worth. 'And that, thankfully, he didn't eat any brains along the way.'

'That's good then, aye,' Tyler said. He realised his smile had fallen away, but he didn't have the energy to fix it back in place.

Snecky was grinning for both of them, anyway. Clearly, he enjoyed his own brand of humour.

'Right, sit down everyone, take your seats,' he eventually said, clapping his hands like he was ushering along a group of primary school children. 'We've got a lot to cover before you lot can knock off for the night.'

Tyler managed to stifle a groan just in the nick of time. Around him, the other new starts took their seats. He squelched ever so slightly as he lowered himself onto the last available chair.

'Yesterday, you may remember, I promised a bit of a treat for all you new recruits. I had hoped to bring in Geoff Palmer, head of the Scene of Crime unit, to both introduce himself and to give you some pointers on how to effectively manage a scene.'

Snecky drew in a deep breath, like he was building up to something big.

'Unfortunately, he shat himself on a bus.'

Tyler laughed. Of course he laughed. How could he not? The statement was so out of the blue, so absurd, that he couldn't not have laughed, even if he'd wanted to.

It was the only sound in the otherwise completely silent room.

'Something amusing, Constable Neish?' Snecky asked, tilting his head back and arching an eyebrow.

Tyler glanced around at the other new starts. None of them met his eye. None of them so much as smirked.

A few of the more experienced officers sitting behind him were clearly battling the urge to laugh, but they were doing a much better job than he was of keeping a lid on it.

'Eh, no, boss. *Sir*, I mean. I just... That was unexpected, is all.'

'I'd imagine it was a bit of a shock for poor Geoff, too,' Snecky said.

Again, Tyler felt the corners of his mouth start to hitch themselves up, but he lowered his head and just nodded, saying nothing.

'I'm sure we all wish him a speedy recovery from whatever gastrointestinal issue he's been afflicted with,' the Chief Inspector continued. 'I'll be sure to pass on your warm regards.'

Tyler raised his head to find Snecky staring, as if daring him to say a word. He did his best to look concerned for the bowel movements of a man he'd never met, and then relaxed a little when the Chief Inspector continued.

'So, I know you'll all be disappointed that Geoff won't be joining us this evening.'

Tyler wasn't disappointed at all. It meant he might get

to knock off twenty minutes earlier than expected, which would only be forty minutes after his shift officially ended.

No such luck.

'But, you'll be pleased to hear that I managed to rustle up an even better guest. Someone you'll likely get to know quite well if you continue to be based here at Burnett Road. Someone who I personally admire a great deal, and who I am certain will have a lot of useful insights to share with you all.'

At the back of the room, the door creaked open. Tyler and the other new recruits all turned in time to see an unkempt man in his early fifties scowling back at them.

'Fuck me,' he declared. 'I haven't clapped eyes on a less appealing bunch since I last squatted over a mirror to scope out my fucking haemorrhoids.'

'Ladies. Gentlemen,' Snecky said, and there was the faintest tremor in his voice that might have been excitement, but might equally have been fear. 'Allow me to introduce you all to Detective Superintendent Robert Hoon.'

CHAPTER
THREE

DETECTIVE SUPERINTENDENT HOON'S speech so far had been short and direct. It would've been a good thirty percent shorter had he taken out the swearing.

Much of it just seemed to be a series of complaints about the police force, the government, and the rest of the world in general. The seven new recruits had all sat at silent attention throughout. To Tyler's surprise, the rest of the room had done the same.

Nobody, it seemed, wanted to end up in this man's bad books.

'I know what you're all thinking,' Hoon continued. There was a slight bulge to his eyes as he glanced from face to face that made him look vaguely demented. 'You're thinking you're the class of twenty-fucking-fifteen, here to blaze a fucking trail. You're thinking you're the good guys. The heroes. The fucking peace-keepers out there righting the wrongs, punishing the guilty. Glorious fucking boys-and-girls-in-blue, saviours to the downtrodden and the oppressed.'

He drew in a breath which, given the way his face contorted, seemed to leave a foul taste in his mouth.

'Are ye fuck,' he declared into the void of terrified silence. 'Get that idea right out of your heads. All you are is glorified babysitters.'

He pointed to the room's only window, the movement so sharp and sudden that it made two of the newbies jump.

'You're the fucking nanny state, making sure the collective herd of brain-dead fucking imbeciles that makes up the general public don't impale themselves on anything sharp, or launch themselves through windscreens, or just collapse under the weight of their own fucking stupidity and ignorance.'

He gave all that just a half-second to sink in, before continuing the rant.

'You are underfunded, understaffed, and—looking at you—woefully under-fucking-qualified for this task. I wouldn't even leave a fucking hamster with some of you, let alone a city full of drunken, horny, dim-witted, bubbling-over-with-repressed-rage, ticking fucking time bombs.'

Snecky, who had been standing a few paces to the side and one back from Hoon with his hands clasped in front of his groin, nodded along deferentially, his eyes darting from recruit to recruit like he was making sure they were all listening.

'You will fail. All of you will fuck this up,' Hoon continued. 'And you will do so again, and again, and again until you die. That's life in the polis, kids. All you can hope for is that you die in your bed when you're old and fucking decrepit, and not because you haven't thought to check that fuckwit you've pulled over for speeding isn't carrying a knife.'

This was, Tyler realised, the first bit of actionable advice the Detective Superintendent had offered since he'd launched into his diatribe. It was about their welfare, too. Maybe he did care, after all.

'Not that it'd put me up nor fucking down, either way,' Hoon said.

Maybe not, then.

The Detective Superintendent checked his watch, muttered something angry sounding below his breath, then started to wrap things up.

'I don't know you lot. I don't fucking want to. If I learn your names, that's a problem, because it means you've been brought to my fucking attention. And believe me, you do not want to be brought to my fucking attention. So, from here on out, this is who you are to me.'

He pointed to the first new recruit, sitting at the opposite end of the front row from Tyler. He was a bigger guy, a full head taller than Tyler, and carrying a bit of extra weight that had made him struggle with some of the fitness stuff during training.

'Dumpling,' Hoon said.

The next recruit was a woman in her early thirties, who fiddled with her hands and kept her head down as Hoon pointed to her.

'Birdy.'

The next man was of average height and average

build. The only thing that immediately distinguished him from the rest of the recruits was the dark brown colour of his skin.

The room collectively held its breath.

'Ginger Tits,' Hoon said, without missing a beat.

The next three were similarly christened.

'Cousin It.'

'Goalie Hands.'

'Fuckly McGee.'

Finally, the Detective Superintendent settled his gaze on Constable Neish.

Tyler ran a hand through his hair. Usually, he kept it buoyed up with an assortment of gels, waxes, and pomades. There was no point doing so when in uniform, though, as the cap flattened it down, negating all the time and effort spent on it. As a result, it sat flat and lifeless on top of his head.

Hoon drew a slow breath in through his nose as he considered the man before him.

'There is literally nothing about you worth fucking commenting on, son,' he announced. 'You're a nothing person. You're like the bastard offspring of a fucking mass-produced shop dummy and a sheet of A4 paper. You barely even fucking exist.'

'Um, cheers, boss,' Tyler said.

Something burned behind Hoon's eyes, making them bulge further. Tyler braced himself for the bollocking to end all bollockings, but the intensity was lessened when Hoon aimed the outburst at the squad in general.

'That's another fucking thing. Don't any of you talk to me. Ever. If you see me in here, out there, anywhere, and your cow-like brains take it upon themselves to form a semi-coherent sentence that you're considering speaking in my direction, don't. Shut that shite down. Stamp that thought to death immediately, and put it out of its fucking misery. I don't want to hear anything you have to say. No words that could come out of your mouth would ever be of any fucking interest to me whatsoever.

'In fact, don't even look at me. The only time you should be making eye contact with me is as a result of an admiration so deeply held that it's changing your fucking sexual identity. And even then, keep it to your fucking self. Alright?'

He nodded without waiting for a response from the group, then set off towards the door.

'Right, that's me,' he declared, only for Chief Inspector Grant to go hurrying after him.

'Uh, sir. Sir, you mind if I have a quick word?'

'I'd object on a fucking number of levels,' Hoon said, not looking back.

'It's, uh, it's about the DCI role in the MIT,' Snecky continued, following Hoon out of the room. He paused just long enough to point to one of the older officers at the back of the room, and then the door pulled closed, and both senior officers were gone.

'Well, he seemed nice,' Tyler muttered. 'Let's hope I never have to deal with that guy again.'

CHAPTER
FOUR

SERGEANT HAWKES, who took over the briefing was, thankfully, no Detective Superintendent Hoon. He wasn't a Chief Inspector Grant, either. There was nothing performative or over the top about his delivery, and he didn't seem on a mission to belittle the new recruits, or make them afraid for their lives. He, like the rest of the officers in the room, just seemed keen to get things over with so he could get home.

He was in his mid-forties, Tyler reckoned, and though he wasn't a kick in the arse off being six foot, he stood with his shoulders slumped like the day, or the job, had taken a toll on him.

'Right, tomorrow, then,' he said, reading from a document Snecky had left on the briefing room table. 'So far, much the same as today. Speed cameras, some welfare checks, someone needs to rifle through some CCTV footage. But we can sort all that in the morning.'

He scanned down the list, a finger tracing down through the lines of text until something caught his eye.

'Oh, and we need a volunteer to be Dinnae.'

'Dinnae?' asked Dumpling at the far end. 'What do you mean, Sarge?'

'Dinnae?' Hawkes said, as if this answered the question. When it was clear that none of the recruits had a clue what he was on about, he clarified. 'Dinnae the Drink-Driving Squirrel. The advert. The posters.'

'Oh, him. Aye,' said Goalie Hands. She sat up a little straighter, like she was expecting to be given an award. 'I've seen the beermats.'

'Well done,' said Hawkes. 'I'll put you down for being in the costume, then. You'll be going pub to pub as part of the Christmas campaign.'

'Nae luck,' Tyler said. He fought back a grin. You wouldn't catch him dead in a costume like that.

'Oh, one other thing here to mention,' Sergeant Hawkes continued, his finger stopping at the very bottom of the list. 'There's a girl been reported missing. Aged sixteen, from out near Culloden. Last seen on the way to school this morning. Never turned up to class.'

'Maybe just jinking,' suggested Ginger Tits.

'Almost certainly. She's got a history of it, according to the parents,' Hawkes said. 'Anyway, she's sixteen. She's run away umpteen times before and always turned up. Chances are she'll be home already, but take one of these and we can circle back if she hasn't shown face by the morning.'

He handed Tyler a small stack of printouts. The image of the girl on the paper was a blurry photocopy of a passport photograph. Even so, Tyler recognised her straight away. A quick glance at the name printed below it confirmed things.

'Laura. Laura Wilder. I know her,' he announced.

'You know a sixteen-year-old lassie?' asked Fuckly McGee, giving him the side-eye.

'Aye. Well, no. Not like... I was in school with her brother. He's a mate of mine. Mumpy.'

'What kind of name's Mumpy?' Sergeant Hawkes asked.

'Eh, just a nickname, Sarge. That's not what his parents called him, or anything,' Tyler replied. 'Real name's Michael. I met Laura a few times. Nice kid. Bit wired to the moon, but... shit. His mum and dad'll be worried.'

Hawkes shrugged. 'Not overly, by the sounds of things. But, you know them?'

Tyler nodded. 'Aye. I used to sleep over now and then. They ran me and Mumpy to school discos and stuff.'

The sergeant put one hand on his lower back and straightened up. He grew an inch or two in height, as if some of the weight had been lifted from his shoulders.

'Good. You can save me a job, then,' he said, handing Tyler another sheet of paper with an address printed on the top. 'You can go round there and take their statement.'

❄

TYLER REGARDED himself in the rear-view mirror of the police car, trying out a few different facial expressions. He was aiming for earnest and capable. Caring, but commanding. The family knew him as 'Wee Tyler', but that wasn't who was about to knock on their door. No, that job belonged to Constable Neish of Police Scotland.

The drive over had been hair-raising enough. He'd driven through Inverness city centre thousands of times before, but never in a police vehicle at rush hour. He'd been terrified of scratching the paintwork, or bumping into another car. He was already going to struggle to live down the Zombie Boy incident without adding an RTA into the mix.

There was supposed to be someone with him. That's what they'd been told during training, at least. For the first few months on the job, all recruits would have a more experienced officer backing them up, showing them the ropes, making sure they didn't mess up too badly.

But as Detective Superintendent Hoon had touched on, Burnett Road was seriously understaffed, and most of the new starts had been thrown in at the deep end and left to get on with it.

'Right, you've got this,' Tyler said, holding his gaze in the mirror. 'You're on top of this. You're the polis.' He raised a finger and pointed to his reflection, stressing that last point. 'You're the bloody polis.'

Then, he winked, blew a kiss, threw open the door, and got out of the car.

His shoes slipped on an icy puddle, and he spent a frantic few seconds waving his arms and yelping, but he grabbed the open car door and steadied himself before he could fully lose his balance.

He didn't bother to look to see if anyone had seen him. It wouldn't help him to know if they had. Instead, he closed the door, smoothed down the front of his high-vis jacket, and set off up the path towards the semi-detached house where Mumpy's parents lived.

He rang the doorbell, took off his cap, and steadied himself.

'Earnest and capable,' he whispered, adjusting his facial features. 'Caring, but commanding.'

Footsteps hurried along the hallway on the other side of the door. Tyler drew himself up to his full, largely unimpressive height.

The door, when it opened, revealed Mumpy. His eyes widened in surprise when he clocked who was standing on the step.

'Tyler?' he asked. He frowned as he saw the expression on the constable's face. 'You alright, mate? You look like you're fucking constipated.'

CHAPTER
FIVE

'OCH, would you look at you! Wee Tyler, all grown up!'

Mumpy's mum, Mrs Wilder, took Tyler's face in her hands and squished his cheeks together. She laughed, showing the slight yellowing of her teeth, and forcing Tyler to inhale the ash on her breath.

She had always been a tall woman, more solidly built than either her son or her husband, and her hands were like a leathery vise gripping Tyler's head.

'He's not grown that much,' Mr Wilder said, appearing from nowhere and slapping Tyler on the back like he was giving him the birthday bumps. 'Did they get rid of the height requirements to be a Bobby? Only way a wee squirt like you could've got in!'

He laughed. His wife laughed. Tyler was suddenly thirteen years old again, eleven, nine, sitting in this same living room, eating cereal in his pyjamas, watching cartoons through the same haze of cigarette smoke that hung in the air.

'They, eh, they have, actually, aye,' Tyler confirmed. 'But I would've made it in anyway. Like, I'd have been the right height even before that.'

As comebacks went, it wasn't exactly a zinger. Mr Wilder patted him on the back again, and Mrs Wilder squidged his cheeks once more, then they both retreated to the armchair and the couch respectively.

'You'll have come about Laura, I take it?' Mr Wilder said.

'Eh, aye. Aye, that's right,' Tyler confirmed.

'Well, you're wasting your time.'

'Oh? Did she turn up?'

Mr Wilder snorted. 'Has she hell. But this is her all over. Bloody drama queen. Isn't she, Mother?'

'Oh, aye. She's that, alright,' Mrs Wilder confirmed.

Tyler had forgotten about Mumpy's dad's tendency to refer to his wife as 'Mother'. It had struck him as odd the first time he'd heard it—she wasn't his mother, after all—but he'd got used to it over time, until it seemed normal.

Now, though, after a break of a few years, it was back to seeming strange again.

'We weren't going to say anything. She'll turn up, like she always does,' Mr Wilder continued. He gestured past Tyler, to where Mumpy was standing with his hands tucked into the front pocket of his faded *Batman* hoodie. 'But this one insisted on phoning it in.'

'I was worried, Dad,' Mumpy said. 'I *am* worried.'

'Och, you've nothing to worry about,' Mrs Wilder assured him. She reached over to a side table and retrieved a cigarette that had been slowly burning down in the ashtray. 'How many times has she done stuff like this? A dozen?'

'More. Twenty. Thirty,' Mr Wilder added. 'She's been running away since she was old enough to reach a bloody door handle. She's like a boomerang, though. She always comes back.'

Mumpy shoved his hands deeper into his pockets. 'No need to sound quite so disappointed,' he muttered, which drew a stern look from his father.

Tyler had always been a bit scared of Mr Wilder. He worked nights through most of Mumpy's childhood, which meant he was usually this mysterious spectre lurking upstairs during the day, and everyone was under orders not to dare disturb him.

It was only after he'd taken early retirement seven or eight years ago that Tyler had spent any real time in his company. He had a sense of humour that was as dry as sandpaper, and could make you feel equally as raw. Despite his wife standing several inches taller than him, he made very clear that he was the man of the house, and his word was law.

Tyler caught Mumpy's eye and offered him a supportive smile. 'Better safe than sorry,' he declared, patting his pockets as he searched for his notebook.

He eventually found it in the back pocket of his trousers, and his pencil tore at the slightly damp pages as he scribbled the time and date.

'Who was the last one to see Laura alive?' he asked.

It was only the look on the family's faces that made him replay that last sentence in his head.

'What do you mean, *alive*?' Mrs Wilder asked.

'Eh, sorry. I didn't mean that. She's alive. I mean, I'm sure she's alive. I don't *know* for sure, obviously, but... I mean, there's no reason to...'

He cleared his throat, looked down at his notebook, and took a moment to compose himself.

'What I meant to ask was, when did you last see Laura?'

Mrs Wilder shot her husband a worried look. He rolled his eyes in return. Behind Tyler, Mumpy muttered, 'For fuck's sake,' below his breath.

Tyler felt his cheeks prickling red. He tucked a finger into the collar of his shirt and tugged on it, giving himself some room to breathe.

'Am I right in thinking it was when she left for school this morning?'

'I saw her then, aye,' Mrs Wilder said. 'She was being a right stroppy cow.'

'No change there, then,' her husband remarked.

'Dad,' Mumpy urged. 'Please.'

Mr Wilder tutted, but said nothing.

'You think something had upset her?' Tyler asked.

'No more than usual,' Mrs Wilder told him. 'She's been a right bloody misery-guts for months now. Hormones, I think. All over the place. Talking back, staying out late, vaping. Have you seen that? This new thing? Vaping? Wee electric tube things, or whatever they are. You get flavours. Vanilla. Fruit. Bloody bubble gum, or what have you.'

She took a long draw on her cigarette, then blew twin plumes of smoke out through her nostrils.

'Bloody dangerous, if you ask me. You don't know what's in them.'

'Right. Have you spoken to her about what might be bothering her?' Tyler asked.

'Oh, good luck with that.' Mrs Wilder chuckled, though there was very little humour in it. 'Takes the face off you if you so much as ask. I'm too old. I wouldn't understand. I don't get it.'

She stubbed the dog-end of the cigarette out in the ashtray, and immediately reached for the packet on the table beside it.

'Like I wasn't out and about at her age, to-ing and fro-ing. We both were, weren't we, Dan?'

'That we were, Mother,' Mr Wilder confirmed. 'I was shagging everything at that age.'

'Jesus, Dad,' Mumpy cried.

'What? Well, I was! We both were! We weren't always just parents, you know? We were teenagers ourselves, so we know what it's like. And we know Laura, and we know she'll be back. So this...' He gestured to Tyler. 'No offence, son, but this is a waste of bloody time. If she's not back by tomorrow, then by all means come in with your wee notebook, then. But mark my words, she'll be home by midnight without so much as a by your leave, or a word of bloody apology.'

TYLER STOOD ON THE STEP, letting the cold, crisp evening air cleanse the smoke from his lungs. Mumpy stepped out after him, glancing back over his shoulder as he pulled the door closed.

'I'm, eh, I'm sorry about that, Ty,' he said. He winced at the thought of the conversation that had just taken place. 'I think they were expecting someone more... experienced.'

'Aye, no worries,' Tyler said, smiling to hide his embarrassment. 'Sorry I said your sister was dead.'

Mumpy laughed, though it sounded hollow.

'Aye, well, hopefully not.'

He rubbed at his forehead and looked off into the night. The frost was a keen one, and tiny flecks of silver danced in the darkness.

'You're worried about her,' Tyler said. 'You think this is different this time.'

Mumpy blew out his cheeks, shrugged, then nodded. 'Maybe. I don't know. Aye. She's been... weird lately.'

'Weird, how?'

'Hiding something, maybe? I don't know. Something's bothered her. She's never exactly forthcoming with stuff. With proper life stuff, I mean. But lately, it's like she doesn't want to talk to us at all. Any of us. Even me.'

Tyler nodded slowly, considering this. Laura was four years younger than her brother, and had always looked up to him. She'd constantly tried to insert herself into whatever games he and Tyler were playing, from *Cowboys and Indians* to *Wii Sports*. Laura's problem had never been saying too little, it had been talking too much.

'You tried phoning her?'

'Of course I've tried phoning her,' said Mumpy. 'We

all have. Phoned, texted. Sent her a message on Facebook. Nothing. She's not even read anything, and the calls have started going straight to voicemail, which she'll never actually check, because she never does.'

'Right. And did she have a boyfriend? Anything like that?' Tyler asked.

'You're doing it again,' Mumpy said. Tyler stared blankly back at him. 'You said, "Did she have a boyfriend?"'

'Does!' Tyler cried. 'Present tense. Does. Shit. Sorry, mate.'

Mumpy shook his head, dismissing the apology. 'Dunno. Not that she ever mentioned. But maybe. Probably. She used to go out a fair bit. I can give you the names of some of her friends, if you like? I mean, I've already called them, but they're not telling me anything. Just saying they haven't seen her. Maybe if it comes from you, though…'

He smirked, despite himself.

'Or, like, a proper policeman…'

'Oi!' Tyler objected, giving him a dunt on the arm.

'Sorry, couldn't resist. Maybe they'll talk to you, though.' Mumpy sighed and wearily shrugged his shoulders. 'Or, maybe the oldies are right, and she'll rock back up in half an hour with a blueberry vape and a bottle of White Lightning.'

'White Lightning. God, them were the days, eh?' Tyler said.

'Aye. Them were the days,' Mumpy confirmed.

He gave Tyler the names and numbers of Laura's friend group, then opened the door.

'It was good to see you again, Ty,' he said, lingering in the doorway.

'Aye, you too, Mumpy.' Tyler slid his notebook into the breast pocket of his jacket, and gave it a tap. 'Leave this with me,' he said. 'Constable Neish is on the case!'

CHAPTER
SIX

TYLER HAD SWUNG BACK to Burnett Road to get changed out of his uniform, and had taken a few minutes to suggest to the duty sergeant that he make some follow-up calls with Laura's friends.

He had been told, in no uncertain terms, that he was not to bloody dare. His job had been done, his mission complete. He was to head home, get some rest, and report back for more of the same bright and early next morning.

He returned home to the smell of marijuana and the staccato roar of gunfire.

'Alright, mate? Busted any heads today?'

'Nah, not so far,' Tyler said, entering the living room and wafting at the smoke. 'What's with the spliff, though? We talked about this.'

Brian, Tyler's flatmate, glanced up from the screen for barely a second. His thumbs continued to work the control pad in his hands. On screen, another player died in a hail of digital lead.

'Did we? When?'

'Every night for the past six months,' Tyler said. He opened a window and tried scooping the smoke towards it, like he was a nightclub bouncer ushering punters towards the exit.

Brian chuckled. 'Oh. Aye. Right enough. Sorry, mate.'

He nipped the end of his joint and sat it in a little round foil tray that had, until recently, contained a *Mr Kipling's* Cherry Bakewell.

'It's just, you know, I'm in the police now,' Tyler continued. 'I can't be going to work stinking of cannabis.'

'Totally, mate. Totally understand. My fault. I'll keep it to my room from now on.'

'Aye, but you said that the last hundred times,' Tyler pointed out.

'No, I know, and that was wrong of me,' Brian said. He looked back at Tyler again, and this time let his gaze linger for a full second. 'It won't happen again, mate. Swear on my mother's life.'

Tyler smiled at that. 'You've killed that poor woman about a dozen times now.'

Brian grinned. 'Aye, well, she's made of stern stuff.' He held out his controller. 'You want a game? This twelve-year-old keeps killing me and screaming at me that I'm his bitch.'

'Well, you probably are his bitch. You're shite at this when you're wasted.'

Brian looked offended. 'What do you mean? Who's wasted? I'm not wasted.'

'You should be, given the smell in this place,' Tyler countered. 'I'm pretty sure the wallpaper'll be tripping balls at this point.'

'What? No! You're the bitch!' Brian bellowed.

The outburst took Tyler by surprise, before he realised his flatmate was shouting into the microphone of his Bluetooth headset.

'Should you no' be in bed anyway, you mouthy wee prick? Go on, I need you fast asleep before I come round there and shag your mum.'

Brian's eyebrows crept higher as he listened to the response in his ear. Tyler could just make out the tinny hissing of the syllables over the sound of gunfire and explosions.

'Where the hell did you learn language like that, young man?' Brian eventually muttered. 'Are you a part-timer in the Merchant Navy, or something?'

He reached for the joint in the ashtray, only for the whole thing to be whipped off the arm of the chair before he could get to it.

'No. Think of your poor mum,' Tyler said, holding the ashtray out of Brian's reach. 'She'll not survive another one. Take it to your room.'

On screen, Brian's character met a violent and untimely death. The words 'GAME OVER' appeared like they'd been daubed on the telly in blood. The cackle of a child's laughter rang out from the headset as Brian tore it off and tossed it onto the floor.

'Fucking kids these days,' he said. He leaned forward, turned off the console, then got to his feet. 'You want tea? I'm making. Did you bring any biscuits?'

'Why would I bring biscuits?' Tyler asked. 'I was at work.'

'I'm sure you passed a biscuit shop on the way home,' Brian said.

Tyler turned to follow him as he headed for the door leading through to the kitchen. To get there, he had to weave his way past an exercise bike, a box of Christmas decorations they hadn't got around to hanging, and a garden gnome that had turned up out of the blue after a recent house party, and which they'd named Mike Baldwin.

'What do you mean?' Tyler asked. 'What's a biscuit shop?'

'A shop that sells biscuits,' Brian said. He looked Tyler up and down as he stood there in his uniform. 'Is this the calibre of detective my tax money pays for?'

'I'm not a detective.'

'Aye, and you never will be with an attitude like that,' Brian reasoned. He tapped him on the head and said, 'Boink.'

'Cheers for that.'

'No worries,' Brian replied. 'Now, tea? Yes, or no?'

'Eh, aye. A quick one. I'll take it through to my room.'

Brian stopped at the kitchen door. 'Oh, right. My company not good enough for you, or something?'

Tyler smirked. 'Well, no. Not really,' he said, then he glanced around like he was worried they were being watched. 'But it's not that. I want to look into something.'

'Is it internet tits?' Brian asked.

'What? No! It's a case,' Tyler whispered, then he

winced at how stupid the word sounded coming out of his mouth. 'You remember Mumpy?'

Brian's forehead furrowed. 'Mumpy Baw Chops from school. Aye, of course I remember. We used to hang out all the time. What about him?'

'I shouldn't say,' Tyler replied.

Brian considered this, then gave a shrug. 'Fair enough.'

'His sister's gone missing,' Tyler said, lunging after him. 'Laura. His wee sister.'

'Missing? That's...' Brian ran a hand down his face. 'Oh, shit. That's not great. That's fucking grim. Any idea where she is?'

'Well, she wouldn't be missing if we knew where she was. She left for school this morning and didn't turn up. Mumpy's worried.'

Furrow lines formed on Brian's brow, like he was struggling to work out a tricky maths problem. Instead, he was wrestling with some long-dormant memory.

'Didn't she use to do that all the time? Run away, I mean. Was that not, like, her thing?'

'Aye. She did, aye,' Tyler confirmed.

'There you go, then. That'll be it. She'll be after the attention, you know what she's like.' Brian yawned. 'Sure she'll turn up.'

Tyler didn't have an argument to offer. Laura *had* done this many times before. Laura did love the attention.

But Mumpy knew that, and he was worried all the same.

'Yeah. Yeah, I'm sure she will,' Tyler agreed.

He thought of the look of concern in his old friend's eyes.

He thought of those names and numbers in his notebook.

'Right, then,' he said, unzipping his jacket. 'You getting that kettle on, or what?'

CHAPTER
SEVEN

JUDGING by the little white floaters, the milk was on the turn. Tyler's customary four sugars masked any sour taste, though, and he sipped away at his tea as he scrolled on his laptop.

Laura's Facebook page was quite sparse. She'd barely posted anything since mid-2014. The only real exception was a photo from a few months ago that showed her and a friend with a filter on that made them look like they had puppy ears and dog noses.

Either side of that, the only updates were related to mobile games that she'd obviously connected to her Facebook account at some point, and a picture of an actor from *The Hunger Games* with the words 'total ride' superimposed across his bare chest.

If there were any clues as to her whereabouts on her profile anywhere, Tyler didn't have the faintest idea of where to start looking.

Maybe there'd be something in her messages, but he

had no way of accessing those. Given that Laura was a sixteen-year-old girl, with a recent trend towards the secretive, he doubted anyone in the Wilder family would know her passwords, either.

Besides, if Mumpy had been able to access the messages and found anything sinister or incriminating, he'd have passed it on, Tyler thought.

Clicking over to Instagram, Tyler searched Laura's name. That brought up a few profiles, and one thumbnail image immediately jumped out at him—a blonde-haired girl pouting at the camera, trout lips on full display.

He clicked the image, only to be met by a message telling him the profile was private. The mouse pointer hovered over the 'request access' button before he thought better of it.

He wasn't supposed to be doing this. He wasn't meant to be getting involved. Snecky would have a field day with him if he found out he'd been carrying out his own investigation. Detective Superintendent Hoon would literally tear him in half and forcibly insert each part into the orifices of the other.

No. He shouldn't get involved. He couldn't.

Besides, Laura's parents and Brian were probably right. She'd turn up, if she hadn't already. This was just something she did.

Tyler's eyes drifted to his notebook sitting on the desk beside him.

He'd been specifically told not to call any of Laura's friends. Calling them would be a very bad idea.

He flicked through the still lightly damp pages until he found the list of names and numbers.

Calling them would be madness.

Calling them was out of the question.

But nobody said anything about searching them.

He punched their names into Facebook and Instagram, trawling through their pages one by one. The Instagram profiles were all just as locked down as Laura's, but a couple of the girls were more active on Facebook.

There were photos from school, from days out, from late nights at the swing park, cradling bottles of *Buckfast* and *Irn Bru*. Laura appeared in a handful of them, pouting alongside the others, like they were all echoes of the same pose.

She was smiling in one photo, holding a vape like it was a big cigar. A wreath of smoke encircled her head, making her hair appear silvery white. Both these things conspired to make her look a bit like the late Jimmy Savile.

Tyler very much doubted that was the vibe she'd have been going for at the time.

In terms of smoking guns, he was drawing a blank. There was nothing here that incriminated anyone, or that indicated where Laura might be.

Tyler had reached a dead end in the limited avenue of investigation that was open to him. Short of driving the streets of Inverness, or risking his job by phoning Laura's mates, there was nothing more he could do tonight.

Still, he didn't want to let Mumpy down. He'd been worried sick, and Tyler had promised him that he was on the case.

Taking another sip of his tea, Tyler flicked his web

browser over to a Google search page. Then, he cracked his knuckles, stretched his neck, and got to work.

TYLER AWOKE with a Post-it Note stuck to his forehead, and the imprint of a pencil sharpener on his left cheek. A string of drool connected him to the desktop, until the voice in his ear made him sit bolt upright.

'You're not dead, then?'

Brian stood beside him, fully dressed in his work overalls and boots, his big waterproof jacket slung over his arm.

'Shit. What?' Tyler peeled the sticky note off his forehead and squinted into the grinning face of his flatmate. 'Did I fall asleep?'

'Looks like it, aye,' Brian said. He gave Tyler's computer mouse a waggle, then bent down to read the text on screen. He almost choked trying to fight back his laughter. '"How to find a missing person,"' he said, reading the words at the top of the page. 'Were you Googling how to be a policeman, Tyler?'

'What, no. Shut up,' Tyler said, suddenly awake. He grabbed the mouse and shut down the browser window. 'I was just… Shit. Wait.'

He stood up suddenly, as a terrible thought occurred to him.

Brian was dressed. Boots on, jacket in hand, ready to head out the door.

'What time is it?'

'Twenty-past eight,' Brian said. 'I'm just heading to the site. Some of us have real jobs to get to.'

What emerged from Tyler's mouth wasn't a word, exactly. It was more like the distant ancestor of a word, emanating from somewhere far deeper and more primal than the voice box.

He was halfway to the door by the time the sound rattled to its conclusion. He didn't hear Brian calling to him until the third or fourth time.

'Tyler. Tyler!'

'What?' Tyler cried, patting himself down as he searched for his keys. 'I'm late! I need to go!'

'I know,' Brian told him. He shot a look at the pile of clothes at the edge of the bed. 'But you might want to take a wee minute to get dressed before you do.'

CHAPTER
EIGHT

TYLER HOPPED into the briefing room, tying a shoe, just as the rest of the new recruits passed him in the opposite direction. The looks they gave him ranged from the largely sympathetic to the positively gleeful.

He appreciated the concerned nods, and couldn't really blame the others for their more gleeful reactions. After all, the more he messed up, the better they'd look by comparison.

'Well. Well. Well.' Chief Inspector Grant stood with his arms folded, tapping a finger on an underdeveloped bicep in time with those three words.

Or one word spoken three times, Tyler supposed.

'What time do we call this, Constable Neish?'

'Eh, just after nine, sir,' Tyler replied, wobbling precariously on one foot as he tied the shoe on the other.

'No,' Snecky said.

Tyler stole a glance at the clock on the wall. It was four

minutes past nine. He'd got to the station and got changed in record time. Technically, today's shift started at nine, and given that he'd done over an hour and a half of unpaid overtime last night, he hoped there might be a little bit of leeway.

'Aye, it is, sir.'

'No. That may be what *you* call it, Constable. What *I* call it is *late for work*,' Snecky said. 'You know you're in the police force now, yes? You know that people rely on you to be where you're meant to be at the time you're meant to be there? You understand that this is part of the arrangement?'

'Yes, sir.'

'That was all explained to you during training?' Snecky continued.

Tyler finished tying his shoe just in time to regain his balance. He stood to attention, and pretended not to notice that his shirttails weren't properly tucked in.

'They did, sir,' he confirmed.

The Chief Inspector wasn't letting this go. 'And you are the owner of a functioning timekeeping device, yes?'

Tyler blinked and had to work quite hard to stifle a yawn. 'Sir?'

'A watch, Constable. You own a watch?'

'Oh, aye. Yes, sir. I've got one of them.'

Snecky stepped in closer, bringing his face in so it was just a few inches away from the constable's. Tyler could hear the air whistling in and out through the other man's long, narrow nose.

'And yet, here we are. Five... no, *six* minutes past nine.'

Tyler thought about pointing out it had only been four minutes past when he'd arrived, but thought better of it.

'I don't want this happening again, Constable. Is that clear?'

Tyler nodded. 'Yes, sir.'

'Because, if it does, you'll see the wrong side of me.' Snecky shot a quick look to the door, then lowered his voice a fraction. 'If you think Detective Superintendent Hoon is scary, you should see me when I'm in full flow. I'd chew him up and spit him out. And I'd do the same to you. You wouldn't want that, would you, Constable?'

Tyler hesitated. 'What, you chewing me up and then spitting me out, sir? No. No, I wouldn't be into that sort of thing.'

Snecky's eyes narrowed. He searched Tyler's face, but found nothing but innocent sincerity there.

'Well, just you keep that in mind,' the Chief Inspector said. He lunged like he was going to throttle the junior officer, then adjusted the collar of his shirt. 'And get yourself tidied up before you head out. You've got a list of welfare checks to do today.'

He stepped back, smirking.

'If any of them seem dead, maybe check for a pulse before calling the ambulance, eh?'

'I'll do my best, sir,' Tyler said.

Snecky waved a hand, dismissing him. Tyler didn't budge. Not yet.

'Any word on the missing girl, sir?'

Snecky appeared puzzled by the question. 'Sorry?'

'Laura Wilder, sir. She was reported missing yesterday morning. Any word of her turning up?'

Tyler was fairly sure he knew the answer already. Mumpy would've texted to let him know if Laura had come home. There had been nothing, though, which meant she was probably still out there somewhere.

'I have absolutely no idea,' Snecky told him. He plucked a printout from a clipboard on the desk, and thrust it out to Constable Neish, pinning it to his chest. 'Welfare checks,' he instructed. 'Knock on doors, make sure they're alright. I struggle to see how even you can mess that up.'

THE DOG WAS GOING to be a problem.

Tyler didn't generally have an issue with the animals. He liked dogs, in fact. He had been likened to a puppy himself a few times, thanks to his bouncy enthusiasm, his big brown eyes, and his occasional tendency to run head-first into stationary objects.

Although, technically, he'd only done that once.

The tricky thing was that, no matter how much Tyler liked dogs, the feeling often didn't seem to be mutual. And that very much appeared to be the case in this instance.

It was Mr Franklin's Alsatian that had first alerted the neighbours to a possible problem. The report that had come in that morning said the dog had been barking since the wee small hours, and nobody had been able to reach Mr Franklin on the phone or at the door.

He was in his eighties, according to the caller. He'd lost his wife to cancer a year back, and hadn't been keeping well since. Normally, though, he'd be out with the dog first thing, and it would trot along beside him as he shuffled his way around the block, stopping only to shite at its usual spot next to the post box.

There had been no sign of movement this morning, though. For the first time in as long as any of those living nearby could remember, Mr Franklin's usual routine had been broken.

Now, Tyler could see the outline of the animal through the dimpled glass of the old man's door. It was a big bastard of a thing, and though the glass mercifully obscured the details of its teeth, it twisted its shape into something that bordered on the monstrous.

Tyler rang the doorbell, then knocked on the glass. Both these things sent the dog into wild spasms of pure fury. Surely, if the old man was alive, all that barking would've woken him up?

Maybe today was the day, then. Maybe this would be Tyler's first dead body.

He found himself hoping not.

'Hello? Mr Franklin? This is the police. Just want to make sure you're OK, sir. Can you come to the door?'

The dog took exception to the sound of Tyler's voice. It began hurtling up and down the hallway, barking and snarling even more furiously than before. If it forgot to stop, it'd come crashing through the glass of the door, which Tyler reckoned probably wouldn't do its mood any favours.

He backed away from the door, and continued around the front of the bungalow. The curtains were drawn in what he guessed was the living room, so he couldn't see inside.

The dog, no longer able to see him through the door, calmed down a bit. Its barking went from three or four a second to one every two seconds. It was definitely an improvement, but it was still getting on Tyler's tits.

He chapped on the window. 'Mr Franklin, you there?'

He listened, closing his eyes to try and better focus his ears.

Nothing.

Well, nothing but the dog.

The next window along was similarly covered. There was a tiny gap at the bottom of the curtains, but the inside of the room was too dark for Tyler to see much. A bedroom, maybe, but he couldn't be sure.

Returning to the front door, he headed up the path, out onto the pavement, and made his way around to the back of the house. Much of yesterday's snow had melted away, but there were still a few pockets back here where the morning sun was yet to reach.

The door to the kitchen was locked. The neighbours had already checked, so this didn't come as any great surprise. The blinds were open back there, revealing a cluttered kitchen with a sink full of stagnant water and dirty dishes. A pile of what looked like dirty laundry lay on the floor near the washing machine, while newspapers lay scattered atop lino that had been chewed at the edges by long, jagged teeth.

The door that connected the kitchen to the hallway was closed. Tyler caught glimpses of movement through the glass as the dog continued to run back and forth, barking its head off.

He should probably call for backup on this one. The dog squad, maybe. Or just someone with more experience of… well, anything.

But he'd been given this job because it was the lowest of the low. He remembered Snecky's parting words, about how even he couldn't mess this up. What would the Chief Inspector say if he couldn't even handle the first name on the list without calling for help?

Tyler put his hands on his hips and considered the kitchen door. It was old, the paint flaking off the weathered wood. He could probably kick it in, if it came to it. He'd never actually attempted that before, but he knew the theory, and it looked easy enough in the movies.

Or maybe it'd be better to put a shoulder to it. He'd have more control that way. Just grab the handle, lower the centre of balance, then *whoomf*, and he'd be in.

He could do that. He could break the door down. No bother.

He stretched his arms, rolled his head around a few times, then took a series of short, shallow breaths.

It was only as he was lining himself up with the door that he noticed the open bathroom window. It was a tall, narrow rectangle, with the same patterned glass as the front door. Just wide enough for him to squeeze through, if he didn't mind shedding his stab vest and some of his dignity.

The safety latch was easy enough for him to reach up and unfasten. The weight of the old window swung it down, and he had to grab for it to stop it slamming closed on his arm.

With a grunt, he pushed it upwards, so it sat horizontally in the frame, exposing the grotty and grubby bathroom beyond. Short shavings of silver hair covered the sink and its surroundings. Mould bloomed on a plasticky white shower curtain that sagged from a rail above a walk-in bath.

And the toilet. Dear God, the toilet. Tyler tried not to look at it, but his sense of smell stepped up to paint a vivid enough picture anyway.

'Aw, Jesus,' he muttered, gulping down some of the outside world's fresh air.

He unzipped his jacket and took off his vest. Inside the house, the dog continued to go bananas.

'I so should've called for backup,' he muttered.

And then, kicking off from the damp grass, he heaved himself up onto the frosty window ledge, and clambered awkwardly in through the gap.

CHAPTER
NINE

IT WAS a relief that no one was around to see his dismount into the bathroom basin. There was a fair amount of clattering, some uncomfortable wriggling, and the odd bit of swearing before Tyler tumbled onto the bathroom floor, landing with a thump that instantly drew the attention of the monster-dog in the hallway.

Being on the floor meant he was dangerously close to what was now clearly a badly blocked toilet. He gagged, bringing tears to his eyes, then hurriedly closed the toilet lid in the hope it would block the worst of the smell.

It didn't.

The door shook in its frame as the Alsatian hurled itself against it. Claws scratched at the wood as the barking rose to fever pitch.

Tyler shot a look back over his shoulder at the window, contemplating climbing straight back out again.

But, no. He'd come this far. There was no backing out now.

A bath towel lay on the floor, damp and musty, and curled up like a snake. Tyler grimaced as he picked it up, then looped it around his forearm several times, creating as much padding as he could for the meat and bone below.

He slapped at the towel a couple of times, checking its protective qualities. All this told him, though, was that should the dog attempt to karate chop him just below the elbow, he'd probably walk away largely unscathed. If it took the more traditional route of using its teeth, however, then the result might be different.

The door shook. The claws scraped. Tyler started to take a deep breath, immediately regretted it, then pulled the door open, thrust his arm out, and braced himself.

The Alsatian stopped barking immediately. At first, Tyler assumed this was because it was unhinging its jaws in order to swallow him whole, but rather than move to attack, it retreated a few paces.

The dog was old, its muzzle a raccoon mask of white and grey. It eyed Tyler warily, and yawned as it tried to shake off all the stress and adrenaline coursing through its muscular body.

'You're alright,' Tyler whispered, keeping the wrapped arm raised. 'You're OK. I'm not going to hurt you.'

He doubted he could, even if he'd wanted to. The dog wasn't quite as supernaturally large as it had seemed through the glass, but it was a solid lump of a thing. One wrong move, and the bastard might still rip his throat out.

As if sensing Tyler's discomfort, the dog shuffled back

and sat down. With a turn of its head, it looked very deliberately along the hallway to its right. Tyler took a couple of cautious, shuffled steps towards it, and followed its gaze.

There was a door. If he had his bearings right, Tyler reckoned it was the second window he'd seen at the front of the house. The one he thought might be a bedroom.

He looked down again to find the dog staring up at him, head slightly tilted to one side like it was waiting for him to get his finger out of his arse and do something.

It continued to watch him as he sidled out of the bathroom, sticking close to the wall, and backed all the way over to the door.

'Mr Franklin?' he called.

The dog's ears twitched, and its head tilted further, but it didn't otherwise react.

Tyler risked a quick knock on the bedroom door. It didn't incite any more barking, or any flash of jagged teeth.

'Mr Franklin, my name's Constable Tyler Neish. I'm with the police. Can I come in?'

There was no response from the other side of the door.

God. Maybe this *was* it. His first dead body. When he finally became a proper copper. The moment he earned his place.

Once again, the dog seemed to read his mind. It let out a low whine and turned its gaze in the direction of the door. Tyler reached for the handle and eased it down. The hinges creaked as he inched the door open, revealing the darkened room beyond.

The smell that rushed out to meet him was stale and sour, like fresh vinegar and old sweat. He took a breath through his mouth and held it as he opened the door the rest of the way.

The light from the hallway spilled into the room, picking its way across discarded clothing and dirty plates until it settled on a double bed in the centre of one wall. A frail, withered figure lay tangled in blankets in the middle of the bed.

Eyes ringed with red shone in the dim light.

'I'm sorry,' a voice sobbed from the shadows. 'I didn't mean to cause anyone any trouble.'

TYLER SAT on an old kitchen chair at the foot of Mr Franklin's bed, watching the old man run a gnarled hand along the length of the Alsatian's back. The dog had come hobbling into the room at the sound of its master's voice, licked his face once, then lay down on the floor beside the bed.

The light was on now, the curtains and window both opened a crack to let some air in. Mr Franklin was still wrapped up in his blankets, his eyes still ringed with red, but from what Tyler could tell, there was nothing that required immediate medical attention, and he *definitely* wasn't dead.

He'd take those wins.

'I'm sorry. I am,' the old man said again. 'I just… I can't do it. I've tried, and I just can't.'

His eyes welled up again, and he wiped them on the arm of his faded tartan pyjamas.

'What can't you do, Mr Franklin?' Tyler asked.

'Any of it. All of it.' The old man gestured around at the room. 'I used to be fine when Ella was here. I'd help out. We'd chip in together. Keep on top of it. I'd do the dinner, she'd wash up, I'd dry. And then… And then she was going to show me the washing machine, but she didn't get the chance, and all the buttons. Have you seen all the buttons? There's so many buttons, and I don't know what they mean.'

His shoulders shook, and he tucked his chin into his chest, screwing his eyes shut like he could hide from his shame. Down on the floor, the dog lowered its head onto its paws and sighed.

'I just can't do it. I can't keep on top of it without her.'

'Hey. Hey, you're alright,' Tyler said, leaning closer and putting a hand on the old man's arm. 'It's fine. It's not too bad. You should see my flat sometimes. It's way worse than this. It's just… It's an emotional time. Run up to Christmas, and that.'

Mr Franklin scowled at the mention of the holiday. 'Och, to hell with Christmas. What's the point without Ella? And I can't keep the house tidy as it is, never mind get it ready for bloody Christmas!'

'You just need a bit of help, that's all,' Tyler told him. 'Do you have family living nearby?'

There was a sniff. A sob. A crack at the back of the throat. 'Just our Sandra.'

'Sandra?' Tyler took out his notebook. 'Is that your daughter, or…?'

The old man opened his eyes. 'What? No. *She's* Sandra. That's her there. The dug.'

'The dog?' Tyler's eyes flitted down to the Alsatian. It stared back at him like it was daring him to say something. 'Sandra. That's... a nice name.'

'It's a bloody ridiculous name for a dug!' Mr Franklin replied, and there was just the slightest note of amusement to it. 'Ella liked it, though, and that was good enough for me.'

He leaned his head back and looked up to the ceiling. His voice shook as he spoke again.

'Oh, I miss her something terrible. If she'd have been here, she'd have battered me black and blue for the state of this place. She always loved this wee hoose. Getting it ready for Christmas and the bells. And look. Look what I've done to it. Look at the mess I've made.'

'It's fine. She'd understand,' Tyler told him. 'I bet she wouldn't want you feeling like this about it, would she?'

Mr Franklin shook his head.

'What would she say to you, d'you think?' Tyler asked. 'If she saw you upset like this?'

The old man thought about this for just a moment. His face lit up into a big beamer of a smile, even as more tears rolled down his cheeks.

'Something wonderful,' he whispered. 'Like she always did.'

Tyler gave the old man's hand another squeeze. 'There you go, then. You hold on to that while I go make us a cup of tea.'

The look of shame returned, wiping the smile from the old man's face. 'I've not got any clean cups.'

Tyler slapped his hands on his thighs as he stood up. 'Aye, well, you leave that to me,' he said. 'I might not have many talents, but I can wash a mean dish.'

The dog raised its head when Tyler left the room, but made no move to follow him. He found his way to the kitchen, filled the kettle and clicked it on, then unlocked the back door and went outside to retrieve his stab-proof vest, with the radio clipped to the shoulder.

He called into base while he rummaged under the sink for some washing-up liquid and something to scrub with. Dispatch listened as he relayed his thoughts on bringing in the paramedics to give the old boy a check over, before confirming that they'd have an ambulance sent round.

'One other thing,' Tyler said, as he tipped the cold, dirty water out of the plastic basin, letting it gurgle down the drain. 'The printout I got says there were calls from three different neighbours. Any chance you can give me their names and addresses?'

CHAPTER
TEN

It took an hour for the ambulance to arrive. By which point, the dishes had been done, the toilet had been unclogged, and the first of the washing was whizzing around inside the machine.

'We didn't know. We didn't realise at all. I feel bloody awful.'

Elaine from two doors down had been the first to call the police that morning, and the first to volunteer to help. She'd feared the worst when Tyler had rocked up at her door, and then gone quiet and misty-eyed when he'd explained the situation.

She'd made a start on the washing. Bill from across the street had sorted the toilet. His wife, Caroline, was off to the shops to buy more cleaning supplies, and Elaine was now doing a full inventory of the cupboards, fridge, and freezer.

'I think things just got on top of him,' Tyler said,

keeping his voice low for fear of the old man hearing and getting embarrassed again.

He'd protested when the neighbours had first rocked up, before his voice had betrayed him and he'd collapsed into soft, throaty sobs. Elaine had popped in to reassure him that they were happy to help, and to lightly reprimand him for not telling them how much he'd been struggling.

He'd started crying on her shoulder then, and Tyler had slipped out of the room to finish with the washing up.

'Eh, you mind taking this dog out of here?' one of the paramedics called from the bedroom. 'It looks like it might try and eat one of us.'

'Or both,' the other medic added.

'She probably needs a walk, anyway,' Elaine said.

She was teetering on a chair, checking dates on the tins in a high cupboard. After a quick glance around the room, she pointed to a lead hanging on the back of the kitchen door.

'There you are. She doesn't go far, just round the block.'

Tyler looked from the woman to the lead and back again. 'Oh, right. You want me to do it?'

'Well, you're the only one standing twiddling his bloody thumbs,' Elaine pointed out. 'And you'll need a poo bag. I've seen the size of what comes out of her, and you're not leaving that lying out on the street.'

❄

'SANDRA, stop! Sandra, whoa! Sandra, slow down!'

Sandra did none of these things. Instead, she continued to drag Tyler on a loop around this part of the housing estate that she had clearly walked a thousand times before.

She had been reluctant to leave her master's side at first, but had been persuaded through the liberal application of biscuits. Once out the door, it was as if some switch had been flicked in her head, and she'd become determined to get the walk over and done with as quickly as caninely possible.

Despite her age, she had an impressive turn of speed, and the strength to ensure that Tyler got dragged along with her.

She led him down the street, and hung a left. This led them alongside the tree-lined grounds of Culloden House Hotel. Not too far from his old stomping ground. Even less so from Mumpy's house.

Technically, Mr Franklin's name hadn't been the first one on the list, but the address had jumped out at him. From here, it was less than a ten-minute walk to the Wilders' home.

Not that Tyler was going to go round there, or anything. He didn't have the time for that, and he certainly didn't have the permission.

But, yeah. Ten minutes. Five if he let Sandra drag him all the way there.

But he couldn't. It was out of the question. He could get into serious trouble.

And besides, it was entirely possible that Laura was back home.

Sandra stopped by a postbox, and sniffed at the ground. While he waited for nature to take its course, Tyler took out his phone, fired off a quick text to Mumpy, and chewed impatiently on his lower lip.

The reply came back almost immediately.

No sign.

'Shite,' Tyler muttered. Which, as it happened, was the one instruction of his that Sandra did actually follow.

As he fished in his pockets for the poo bag, Tyler got back on his radio to base.

'Um, sorry, I'm stuck at that Culloden address with Mr Franklin. Can you get someone else to handle the rest of these welfare checks for me?' he asked.

He turned and looked to his right, past the entrance to the housing estate, past the hotel grounds, and off towards the building that lay beyond. The building where he, Mumpy, and a couple of thousand other kids had spent most of their teenage years.

'This one's going to take a little bit longer than I thought.'

'Mrs M!'

Mrs Morrison, Tyler's fourth-year Chemistry teacher, stopped halfway between her car and the school gate. She looked around for whoever had spoken, then stared at

Tyler for several seconds, her slowly dawning recognition gradually tipping over into something more like horror.

'Tyler? Tyler Neish?'

'The one and only, Miss!' Tyler declared, holding his arms out at his sides like he was presenting himself as a raffle prize.

The teacher rushed over to him, head tick-tocking from side to side, like she was scanning for danger.

'What the hell are you doing, Tyler? You can't wear that! You'll get into trouble!'

The lower half of Tyler's face remained fixed in a smile, but the top half settled into a look of confusion.

'What?'

'You can't dress up like a policeman. You'll get arrested,' Mrs Morrison hissed. A terrible thought occurred to her, and she took a sudden step back. 'You're not a stripper, are you? That's not what this is?'

'No! No, I'm not a... I'm in the police. I'm a police officer.'

Mrs M was one of those teachers whose age was impossible to guess. Fifty, maybe? Sixty? Seventy wasn't entirely out of the question. Based on the class photos in the school foyer, she'd had the same bob of grey hair for at least two decades.

'The police?' she asked. She looked him up and down. If anything, she looked even more horrified than she had just a moment before. 'The police police? The actual police?'

Tyler nodded. 'Aye.'

'The *proper* police?'

'Yes, Miss. The proper actual police.'

'Not a security guard, or something?'

'No. The actual real police. Look.' He pointed to the insignia on his hat. 'I'm a constable. Just started a couple of weeks back, so, you know, early days.'

The horror in Mrs Morrison's eyes was making him uncomfortable. He clicked his fingers and danced on the spot, his mouth switching into autopilot as it tried to fill the awkward silence.

'What about you? What are you up to these days?'

Mrs M turned her head slowly in the direction of the enormous secondary school standing behind her. 'Teaching,' she said. 'In there.'

Tyler laughed. 'Right! Aye. I mean, yes. Obviously. That makes sense. Because, you know, you're here, and you've been doing it for, like, forever.'

'I wouldn't say *forever*,' the teacher objected.

'No. Well, no. I didn't mean…'

Tyler wished he still had Sandra with him. He could have pretended to lose his grip on her lead so he could go racing after her. It would've been a useful way of escaping this conversation.

But he'd brought her back home, then spent twenty minutes making sure things were ticking along in Mr Franklin's house. More neighbours had come to join the clean-up effort, and the place had been a hive of activity when Tyler had finally said his farewells.

The old man had apologised again, then shaken his hand and thanked him. It had been far and away Tyler's favourite moment of his career to-date.

Although, admittedly, there wasn't yet much in the way of competition.

'Is there something I can do for you, Tyler?' Mrs Morrison asked. 'Break's going to be over shortly, and I need to get back inside.'

'Oh. Right. Aye. No. I mean, yes. Aye. Maybe,' Tyler said.

'That's a lot of words to say nothing,' the teacher pointed out.

Tyler felt his cheeks redden. Suddenly, he was fourteen or fifteen again, being called out for trying to impress the girls in his class.

'Sorry, aye,' he said, pulling himself together. 'I'm looking into Laura Wilder. I believe she didn't turn up for school yesterday morning.'

Mrs Morrison's expression didn't change. 'I don't think I know her. She's not one of mine. Reception will be able to check if she turned up today.'

'I don't reckon she will have, but I can check,' Tyler said. 'But that's not the reason I'm here.'

He reached into his pocket, took out his notebook, and presented the list of names he'd scribbled down the night before.

'I was actually hoping I could have a quick word with these girls.'

'DON'T WORRY, girls, none of you are in any sort of trouble.'

Tyler flashed one of his friendlier smiles at the group standing huddled in a corner of the schoolyard, puffing on vapes out of sight of the main building.

There were three of them, aged between sixteen and seventeen, though they all looked more mature. His age, maybe even a year or two older.

'What if I want to get into trouble, but?' asked one of the girls. Lana, Tyler thought, based on the description Mrs Morrison had given. 'Would you handcuff me?'

'What? No. I don't think that's—'

'What if we were really bad, though?' another of the girls asked. Melissa or Cody. Tyler hadn't yet figured out which was which. She put her hands above her head, wrists touching. 'Would you cuff us like this?' She brought both hands behind her back and leaned forward a little. 'Or like this?'

Tyler had to clench his jaw to keep his smile fixed in place.

'Aye, very good,' he said. 'Handcuffs, uniform, blah, blah, blah. Funny stuff. You got it out of your system?'

'Aye, shut up, Cody,' the third girl said. 'You're such a slag.'

'It was a joke!' Cody shot back. She rolled her eyes so forcefully they almost did a full loop-de-loop, then shoved her vape in the side of her mouth and sucked aggressively on it.

'It was a shite joke,' Lana said, only for Cody to round on her, too.

'You fucking started it! I was just joining it.'

'That's 'cause I'm a trendsetter and you're a sheep,' Lana said, with a haughty toss of her hair that suggested the argument had been won. She turned her attention back to Tyler. 'Sorry about her. She's a total slag.'

'I'm not a slag!' Cody protested.

'Aye, you are,' Melissa countered. 'Danny in Sixth Year said you've been banged more often than Stevie Wonder's big toe.' She took a draw on her vape, then blew out a big cloud of white vapour. 'I mean, I don't know who that is, but he said it was really funny.'

'Aye, well, Danny's a weirdo,' Cody spat. 'He's into Kate Bush, and his knees go in different directions.'

'That's genetic!' Melissa cried, squaring up to the girl beside her. 'He can't help that!'

'What, his knees or Kate Bush?' asked Lana. She was completely straight-faced, and Tyler honestly couldn't tell if the question was serious or not.

'I'm looking for Laura,' he said, raising his voice to cut through their bickering.

The girls stopped arguing, and all turned to him as one, eyes narrowing, vapes raising to their lips. A united front of silence.

'She's not in trouble either. I just... Her family's worried about her. She's not been home all night. Nobody's seen her since yesterday morning. I'm just... I'm scared something's happened to her. I want to make sure she's OK.'

All three girls folded their arms across the front of their uniforms. Despite the cold, none of them had a jacket. In fact, only two or three of the hundreds of kids he'd passed while looking for the girls wore coats of any kind.

Kids were bloody idiots.

Of course, he hadn't worn a jacket throughout his entire time at the school, either, because jackets were for losers. But that was a different time. He was sure the weather had felt much milder back then.

'Have you heard from her?' he pressed. 'A call, a text? Seen anything on her social media, or… Just anything that might help find her?'

It was Melissa who cracked first.

'No. Nothing.'

'I mean, ugh, she wouldn't phone anyway, she's not, like, a complete psycho,' Cody explained. 'But she's not reading her Snaps.'

Tyler frowned. 'Snaps?'

'Aye, Snaps. Like, on Snapchat,' Lana said, in a tone that suggested he was offensively stupid for not knowing this. 'She's not even seeing them.'

Tyler nodded as he processed this information. 'Right. And when she ran away before, did she keep in touch?'

'Constantly,' Cody said.

'All the time,' Melissa agreed. 'Like, we had group chats, and she'd give us the blow-by-blow. Where she was, what she was doing, when she was coming back. All of it.'

'It was mental,' Cody concluded. 'Funny as, like, but mental. Like, mental hilarious.'

'Aye, totally mental hilarious,' Lana confirmed.

The girls all puffed on their vapes in unison. Tyler rubbed at his forehead, trying to fend off the headache he could already feel building. A dozen or so other pupils had slowed while passing, and now stood watching the conversation from twenty yards away.

They were going to draw the attention of a teacher. Mrs Morrison hadn't been that bothered about him wandering through the school grounds, but if anyone more senior spotted him, they might get in touch with the station, and that would be very bad news for Tyler's career.

'So, you don't know where she is? What about recently? Has she been acting differently? She been talking about anyone new?'

The girls' mouths remained shut, aside from a tiny slot at the corner where their vapes went.

'Come on, I'm trying to help her here,' Tyler pleaded. 'I'm not just a cop, I'm a friend of the family. I was in school with her brother, Michael. I used to hang out at the house all the time. I know Laura, she knows me.'

'Holy shit, are you him?' Cody cried. 'Are you her brother's mate?'

Tyler hesitated. 'Um, aye. Maybe. I mean, yeah.'

'The one she fancied?'

'What? No. No, I don't think—'

'Aye, you are! I bet he is!' Melissa said. 'I bet you're the one she had a crush on since she was eight.'

Tyler shook his head. 'No. No, I don't think that's…'

'She used to talk about you all the time. Totally fancied the arse off you,' Lana said, chiming in with the others.

'You sure you've not taken her?' Cody cackled. 'For a bit of—'

'That's enough,' Tyler snapped, and the sharpness of it cut the chatter dead. 'My mate's wee sister, your friend, is missing. Nobody has any idea where she is, or what's happened to her. If you care about her, if you really are her mates, then you'll cut the shit, drop the attitude, and tell me whatever you know, so that maybe I can find her and bring her home.'

He eyeballed all three of them in turn, like he was daring them to play up. Not one of them uttered a word.

'Good. Right. So, as I was saying, has she changed recently? Started doing anything out of the ordinary? Hanging out with anyone new?'

'Yeah,' Cody said.

'Which one?' Tyler asked.

'All of them. She's been weird for months. Started being all, like, happy and stuff.'

'And then miserable,' Lana added.

'So fucking miserable,' Melissa confirmed.

'And new people?' Tyler urged. 'Has she been hanging out with someone different?'

All three girls nodded.

'Who?'

Looks were exchanged. Agreements were reached in silence.

Cody raised a hand and extended a finger. 'Him.'

Tyler turned, following the finger. A tall, skinny lad with trousers that didn't quite reach all the way to the top of his socks stood frozen like a deer in headlights.

'Callum McPhee,' Lana said.

'He walked her home from school the day before yesterday,' added Melissa.

'Right,' Tyler began.

The word was like a shot from a starting pistol. Callum, who had been looking increasingly uncomfortable from the moment Cody had pointed in his direction, turned and shot off, his long legs powering him across the schoolyard in the direction of the main gates.

'Shit. *Shit*,' Tyler ejected.

He glanced back at the girls. He took in all the startled faces of the pupils gathered nearby. A couple of teachers were poking their heads out of the staffroom window, trying to get a look at what was going on.

'Ah, fuck it,' Tyler muttered.

And with that, he ran.

CHAPTER
ELEVEN

TYLER SUSPECTED that this was going to play a significant part in his police career. Running. Running towards things, he hoped, more than running away from them, though he couldn't rule out the latter.

That was assuming that he still had a police career, of course. He was just a few weeks into the job, and going against a direct order. Not only that, he'd just chased a gangly sixteen-year-old off of school property, and was continuing in hot pursuit.

Callum hadn't looked particularly athletic when Tyler had first clapped eyes on him, but by God, he had produced a fair turn of speed. He galloped along on his long, spindly legs, the icy pavement flying by beneath his feet.

He was across the road in a flash, darting in front of a car that blasted its horn and screeched on its brakes. It stopped directly in Tyler's path, and though he briefly contemplated sliding stylishly across the bonnet, he decided that running around it was much less likely to result in injury.

'Callum, stop!' he roared, as the boy plunged through a gap in the trees and vaulted the fence. He stumbled as he landed, then set off at a sprint across an open field dotted with patches of snow that formed part of the grounds of Culloden House Hotel.

If Callum heard him, he didn't let on. He just lowered his head and threw himself onwards, covering the terrain in giant leaps and bounds.

'What is he, an Olympic sprinter or something?' Tyler wheezed. He threw himself over the fence, rolled awkwardly, then sprang back to his feet and continued the pursuit.

'Callum, I just want to talk to you!' Tyler bellowed, but the boy either wasn't listening, or wasn't in a chatty mood. He powered on, pulling ahead, already halfway across the field and closing on the fence that separated the hotel grounds from a neighbouring housing estate.

If he made it there, Tyler would lose him, he was sure of it. Yes, he could probably get an address from the school, but that would make things official. That would flag all this to the attention of the senior officers back at Burnett Road.

And Tyler really didn't want that to happen. Not yet, anyway. Not until he had information that might bring Laura safely back home.

Digging deep, he leaned forward, tucked in his elbows, and forced his legs to move faster. The icy December air nipped at his skin and brought tears to his eyes.

Ignore it, he thought. *Fight through.*

All that mattered was catching up with Callum and finding out what he knew. All that mattered was finding Laura alive.

Everything else would just have to wait.

One thing that definitely wasn't prepared to wait, though, was Callum. He had already reached the fence, and fired a look back over his shoulder as he went bounding towards it like a hurdler.

The look back was his big mistake. He was still in the process of facing front again when he started to make his jump. The timing was off, though, and rather than clear the top of the fence, the whole of his foot slipped into one of the squares of steel wire just a few inches below.

The unstoppable force of Callum's momentum met the immovable object of a two-hundred-metre-long metal fence, and immediately came off second best.

For a brief, glorious moment, Callum seemed to hang there in mid-air, before the anchor point of his foot and the application of basic physics slammed him onto the grassy verge on the other side.

Tyler grimaced. 'Ooh, shit!'

Callum had hit the ground hard, and now lay there, face down on the grass, not moving, his foot still snared in the fence.

Oh no.

Not this.

Don't let *this* be his first dead body.

Tyler sighed with relief when Callum's stunned moment of silence gave way to a cry of shock and pain. The boy thrashed his foot around, trying to free himself, but Tyler had already closed the gap. He vaulted the fence, took a moment to get his breath back, then squatted down by Callum's side.

'Now, then,' he said between wheezes. 'You mind telling me just what the hell that was all about?'

To Tyler's immense relief, Callum had no broken bones or other obvious injuries. The way he'd pivoted on that foot had nearly sent Tyler's stomach dropping out through his arse. Explaining why he'd been chasing a teenager when he was supposed to be on a welfare check would be difficult enough. That teenager having a shattered ankle or a full-blown concussion would only complicate things further.

But, while Callum was physically undamaged, the same couldn't be said for his emotional state. He had started sobbing almost as soon as Tyler had spoken to him. Not crying. Not weeping. An epic, full-scale meltdown like he'd just witnessed his entire family being shot dead before his eyes.

The wailing and howling echoed off the houses that lined the street around them. Tyler held a hand out, trying to console him.

'Hey, you're alright. Deep breaths, Callum. Calm down, OK?'

The boy choked out a reply, each word punctuated by a shaky intake of breath.

'I... didn't... do... nothing.'

'OK. OK, cool. That's good. Glad to hear it,' Tyler said.

'Don't… put me… in… jail.'

'I don't plan to. I just want to talk, that's all. If you hadn't run away, we'd just have had a quick chat at school, that's all.'

This only seemed to upset the boy more. He screwed up his face, squeezing out more tears and silvery strands of snot. The breaths between words became gasps and hiccups.

'My… dad'll… kill… me.'

'I'm not going to say anything to your dad,' Tyler assured him. 'I've just got a couple of questions, then I can walk you back to school.'

He held a hand out to the boy and smiled.

'How does that sound?'

Callum's bottom lip trembled as he considered the outstretched hand. He bubbled and bawled for a few more moments, then accepted Tyler's help to get back to his feet.

As Tyler helped the boy up, he caught a glimpse of a red mark on the inside of his forearm, just past the wrist. Callum saw him clocking it, and hurriedly adjusted his sleeve.

He stole a look along the street on his left, as if he was considering making another run for it. Tyler released his hand, but readied himself to give chase all over again.

Thankfully, it didn't come to that.

'What is it you want to ask me about?' Callum whispered, wiping his face on the sleeve of his school jumper.

Like most of the other kids at the school, he wasn't wearing any sort of jacket. Given the draft that must be shooting up the legs of his trousers, the boy was probably freezing. He was certainly shivering, anyway, although that might have been the adrenaline.

'Is it about Laura?'

Tyler nodded. 'Aye. Her friends said you walked her home the other night. That true?'

Callum shuffled awkwardly on the spot, and gave a little shrug of his shoulders.

'You don't know? What do you mean? Either you did, or you didn't.'

'I did. For a bit. Just, like, some of the way,' Callum said. 'But not… just like, as friends. Nothing else.'

'OK. That's cool. That's nice of you. It's dark early. Very gentlemanly,' Tyler said.

He looked at the houses around them. A few of them were decorated for Christmas, with lights already twinkling, and an inflatable Santa fastened to one of the chimneys.

'Do you live down this way?'

Callum danced from foot to foot again, then nodded.

'Quite out of the way from Laura's house,' Tyler noted. 'Opposite direction, really. She must be a good friend.'

'We went to primary school together,' Callum explained. 'She's… I don't know. A laugh.'

'Nice one. Do you hang out often?'

Callum shook his head. 'Not really.'

'Would you like to?'

The boy met Tyler's eye, just for a second, maybe less. He shrugged. 'Dunno. Yeah. Suppose.'

'You walk her all the way home?'

'Just to the end of her street. I had to get back before my dad got home from work. I do our dinner.'

'Mum not around?' Tyler asked.

Callum gave a single shake of his head, and fiddled with his fingers.

'Sorry to hear that.'

'People make fun of me because she's not around,' Callum mumbled. 'Not Laura, though.'

'She's a good kid,' Tyler said. 'I know her family. I like her a lot. I really want to bring her home.' He positioned himself so that Callum had no choice but to look him in the eye. 'Do you have any idea where she might be?'

'No.'

'She didn't say anything to you? You haven't seen her around?'

'No.'

'Or, I don't know, helped her hide somewhere, maybe?'

'What? No!'

'What happened to your arm, Callum?'

Callum's eyes widened. He slapped a hand on his sleeve, pinning it in place. 'Nothing.'

'Looked like a scratch,' Tyler told him.

'I'm fine.'

'You mind if I take a look at it?'

'I said I'm fine!' Callum cried. He began marching along the street. Though there was a suggestion of a limp to start with, it passed quickly. 'I need to go.'

'Callum, wait,' Tyler urged. 'I just want to find her. I just want to know she's OK.'

'I don't know anything!'

'Then talk to me.'

'I don't know where she is!'

'You were the last one of her friends to see her.'

Callum stopped. Turned. Roared his next words in Tyler's direction.

'She said she was going to leave him for me! Why would I do anything to hurt her? She said once she'd told him it was over, then I could be her boyfriend!'

The outburst rang in Tyler's ears long after its echo had faded. He spoke quietly, cautiously, in case he startled the trembling boy and made him run again.

'Leave who for you, Callum?' he asked. 'Who was Laura planning on breaking up with?'

CHAPTER
TWELVE

'WHO'S THAT CREEPY-LOOKING BASTARD?'

Tyler almost jumped off the couch in fright as Brian leaned down behind him.

'Joint!' he said, which prompted an apologetic look and some frantic hand waving from his flatmate.

'Shit. Sorry. Forgot I had that,' Brian said, nipping the end of the roll-up and tucking it behind his ear. He nodded to the phone in Tyler's hand. 'Who's your man?'

'Dunno,' Tyler admitted.

'Why are you ogling him, then?'

'I'm not ogling him. It's a...' Tyler shifted uncomfortably on the cushion, before eventually muttering, 'Clue.'

'A clue?' Brian ruffled Tyler's hair. This was annoying, as it had taken Tyler a good twenty minutes to get it sitting right after his shower. 'Check you out, Sherlock Holmes. Gay Sherlock Holmes. Sherlock Homo.'

Tyler sighed. 'I'm not gay.'

'Aye, you keep telling yourself that, bud,' Brian said.

'I'm not. I mean, not that there'd be anything wrong with it if I was, but—'

'Shh.' Brian placed a finger on Tyler's lips. 'Live your truth, Ty. Don't let anyone take that away from you.'

Despite himself, Tyler smirked. 'You're such a dick.'

'Aye, but not as much as him. Who is he?' Brian asked, indicating the photo again. 'That's Mumpy's wee sister, isn't it?'

'Yeah. And I'm not sure who he is. A boyfriend, maybe.'

'A boyfriend? He looks about thirty.' Brian held out his hand for the phone, then pinch-zoomed in on the man's face. 'Mind you, look at that 'tache. That's a pure paedo *stash* if ever I saw one.'

He zoomed out again, and spent several seconds studying the image before Tyler eventually took the phone back.

'Where'd you get it from?'

'Laura's Instagram,' Tyler replied. 'A boy from her school took a screenshot for me, but he didn't know a name, or where the picture was taken, or anything.'

'What about the wee bit? Anything in there?'

Tyler turned to look back at his flatmate. 'What wee bit?'

'The wee bit. Underneath. Down the bottom,' Brian explained. He tutted at Tyler's blank look. 'Fuck's sake. The text bit. Where you write stuff! The bit. The wee fucking bit!'

'Alright, calm down!' Tyler cried. 'No. There's nothing

in the wee bit. Nothing helpful, anyway. Just says "Hanging out."'

Brian straightened up. 'Well, that tells us nothing. You sent this to Mumpy?'

'Aye.'

'And?'

'He's got no idea. Never seen him before. He's going to ask around a few folk, though. Talk to Laura's friends. Not sure they'll be much help, mind you. I spoke to them already today.'

'Aye? How did that go?' Brian asked.

Tyler blew out his cheeks. 'I want to say fine, but it was mostly just terrifying. Girls that age are mental.'

'Girls any age are mental, mate,' Brian said. He gave Tyler a nudge. 'That's why you're right not to get involved.'

Tyler chose not to respond to yet another gay jibe. He just stared at the picture on screen instead, like if he looked long enough, the man's name might just spontaneously pop into his head.

He'd tried to bring Laura's disappearance up with Sergeant Hawkes when he'd returned to the station, but had once again been given short shrift. She was healthy, streetwise, technically an adult, and was flagged on the systems as being a repeat runaway who had safely returned home of her own free will several times over the past few years.

It had been less than thirty-six hours since she'd last been seen, and given how short-staffed the station was, she was being treated as low risk and low priority.

If she still hadn't turned up in a day or two, maybe

some resources could be assigned to investigate, but even then, there were no guarantees.

'I should have shown them the photo,' Tyler said.

'Showed who?' Brian asked.

'The sarge. The Chief Inspector. I don't know. Someone. Maybe they'd take it more seriously if they knew she had an older boyfriend. Maybe they could identify him from the photo.'

'Why didn't you?'

Tyler groaned and rubbed at his forehead. The screen of his phone dimmed, so Laura and her mystery man were swallowed by the darkness.

'I wasn't meant to be looking into it,' Tyler admitted. 'I sort of chased a kid for half a mile and nearly broke his leg. That's the only reason I've got this.'

'Fucking hell, Ty. That's hardcore,' Brian said, patting him on the shoulder. 'But, I can see how it might be a problem, right enough.'

'I know. But I should still say something, shouldn't I? Something could've happened to her. This guy might know something.'

'I'm sure she's fine, mate,' Brian countered.

Tyler nodded, even though he wasn't.

'You said Mumpy's asking round, aye?' Brian continued. 'So, see what he finds out. Leave it tonight. If she hasn't turned up tomorrow, bring this to your boss then. Tell him Mumpy sent it to you. Make something up.'

'You think?'

'Here, this is me you're talking to. When have I ever steered you wrong?'

'Joint,' Tyler said.

Brian looked down at the roll-up that he'd stuck between his lips without realising, and was in the process of trying to light.

'Oh. Shite. Aye. Force of habit,' he said, replacing it back behind his ear. 'Now, I'm off out with the boys.'

Tyler leaned forward so he could fully turn to look back at his flatmate.

'What boys?'

'From work. From the yard. The boys. Edgar. Big Gary. Moobs. It's our Christmas night out.' He hesitated, like he was wrestling with his conscience. 'You can come if you want. Just, you know, lay off the cop chat. Some of the boys aren't exactly on speaking terms with the old Five-O. Especially Moobs.'

Tyler gave the offer some thought, though not much. 'Nah, you're fine. Cheers, though.'

'You sure? Might do you good to go out and get pished. Maybe you could meet someone. A man. A nice wee gay man.'

Tyler rolled his eyes. 'I'll give it a miss. I've got work early.'

'So have we,' Brian pointed out. 'Proper work. Man's work. Not chasing wee boys and breaking their legs.'

'Yeah, yeah,' Tyler said, settling back onto the couch. 'Enjoy your night. Try and not bring a party back.'

'No promises,' Brian said. He leaned down again, resting his weight on the back of the couch. 'Here, show us your man again.'

Tyler pressed the button that woke up his phone screen. Brian made a show of staring at the mystery man, then pointed at his own eyes with two fingers, before aiming them at the screen.

'I'll keep the old peepers peeled.' He stood up and ruffled Tyler's hair, messing it up all over again. 'And if I see the dirty bastard, I'll wrap him up for you, and bring him home.'

CHAPTER
THIRTEEN

THIS TIME, Tyler remembered to set the alarm. Not that he needed it. He'd spent half the night awake, braced for the inevitable chaos of whatever drunken group Brian dragged back to the flat.

For once, though, Tyler's flatmate was as good as his word. His key had scraped at the lock around half two in the morning, then he'd spent twenty minutes clattering around in the kitchen making himself something to eat, before heading through to his bed.

Mere seconds had passed between the sound of his mattress creaking, and the low rumble of his snoring.

After that, Tyler's mind had just whirred with thoughts of Laura, and Mumpy, and the mystery man in that photograph.

He should've said something yesterday. He should've gone to Chief Inspector Grant, told him what he'd found, forced him to listen.

He'd probably be out of a job by now, if he had, but

maybe they'd be a step closer to finding the girl. And, as hard as he'd worked to get even this far in the force, bringing Laura home was more important.

There had been nothing back from Mumpy, even after Tyler had rattled off a text asking for an update. Presumably, then, Laura's friends hadn't proven helpful. Which meant that either they didn't know who the man in the photo was, or they were protecting someone.

Worrying about Laura eventually gave way to worrying about the upcoming alarm. With three hours to go until it was due to go off, Tyler became concerned he was going to sleep through it.

At two hours to go, he was fully convinced he'd miss it.

At one hour, he'd decided that what little sleep was left wasn't worth the risk, and had dragged himself out of bed and into the shower.

Brian was waiting at the bathroom door when Tyler finally emerged.

'Morning,' the flatmate grunted.

'Alright? How was your night?'

Brian shrugged. 'Fine, aye. Nothing that exciting. We didn't want to tan the arse out of it when we had work in the morning.'

Tyler made a show of looking surprised. 'Bloody hell. You lot growing up at last?'

Brian gave him the finger. 'Nah, just saving it up for Mad Friday on Friday.'

'Oh, is Mad Friday on a Friday this year?' Tyler asked. 'That's a twist.'

Brian brought up the other hand, the same finger raised.

'Funny. Now, are you going to shift out the road? Or am I going to take a shite right here in the hall?'

TYLER DIDN'T MENTION Laura once during Sergeant Hawkes' morning briefing. Nor, for that matter, did anyone else.

He sat in silence on the front row, one hand pressed on his knee to stop his leg from bouncing, as Hawked assigned all the new recruits their tasks for the day.

Tyler was going to be out on the A9 with a speed camera all day. It was better than being in the big squirrel suit, but he'd have preferred another day of welfare checks.

The fact that he'd only managed one the day before likely meant it'd be a long time before he was given that particular task again.

'This one's for the rest of you,' Hawkes said, looking past the newbies to the older hands sitting behind. 'There are plans being formulated for a raid on Bosco Maximuke between Christmas and Hogmanay. All the local builders and their yards are shut down now until the new year, and his should be no exception.

'If you're passing one of his yards or sites, and you see activity of any kind, record and report. Don't get involved, don't draw attention to yourself. Record, report, and get the hell out of there. Everything'll be passed on to CID with your name attached, so if you're trying to make a good impression, keep your eyes open.'

A hand went up in the front row. Tyler had to bite his tongue to stop his impatience from getting the better of him. He'd called Mumpy earlier, and there was still no word from Laura. She'd been missing for two straight days, and they were no closer to finding her.

'Yes?' Hawkes asked.

Dumpling, the hefty lad at the opposite end of the row, lowered his hand again. 'Who's Bosco Maximuke?'

'None of your concern, that's who,' the sergeant said. 'You're wrangling an oversized squirrel today, Constable. That's all you need to worry yourself about.'

He looked out at the sea of uniforms.

'Now, if nobody else has anything to add…'

Tyler was already up on his feet.

'Let's go out there and get to work.'

CHAPTER
FOURTEEN

'ENTER!'

Tyler recited a quick affirmative mantra in his head— '*Don't fuck this up*'—then pushed open the door to Chief Inspector Grant's office.

Snecky was perched behind his desk, which sat slap bang in the centre of his office. The office itself was tucked away up the back of the bullpen, and Tyler had been forced to stride past constables and sergeants alike on his way to the CI's door.

Large windows looked out onto the rest of the squad, but Snecky had drawn the blinds, cutting him off from everyone. Although, Tyler noted, there were a couple of wee gaps where he could peek out, if he wanted.

The office itself was impeccably tidy. It was the tidiest room Tyler had seen in the whole of Burnett Station, in fact. The desk was completely clear of paper-work. Three filing cabinets lined the back walls, and they were made conspicuous by the lack of papers and folders balanced on top of them, waiting to be filed away.

It felt more like an example of a room than an actual one. If IKEA had started a Police Scotland furniture range, Snecky's office could've been their flagship display.

It was a room for sitting in, not working in. Or for hiding in, maybe.

'Aha. Constable...' Snecky clicked his fingers twice, like he was summoning a long-suffering servant.

'Neish, sir.'

'Constable Neish!' The CI smiled and pointed. 'Taylor.'

'Tyler.'

'Tyler!' Snecky grinned and drummed his hands on the desk, like he'd hit the jackpot. 'Constable Tyler Neish! In the flesh. What can I do for you?'

'Uh, sorry to bother you, sir,' Tyler began, but a shake of the head and a waggled finger from Snecky silenced him.

'I said at the start of last week that my door was always open, did I not?'

'You did, sir,' Tyler confirmed.

Snecky glanced past him, his smile waning just a fraction. 'I mean, it wasn't, obviously. It was closed, and I was in the middle of something. But you weren't to know that. And I did say. Did I not?'

Tyler wasn't sure if the question was rhetorical this time. When Snecky continued to stare at him, he decided it probably wasn't.

'You did say, sir, yes,' he confirmed for a second time.

'Good. And it's handy you're here, actually. I could use your help with something.'

He drummed his hands on the desk again, then stood up. He was dressed in full office uniform—white shirt, black tie, black trousers with a crisp line ironed down the front, and shoes so polished you could see your open pores in them.

As he stood, he adjusted the epaulettes on his shoulder, and Tyler got the impression he was showing off the three pips that marked his rank.

'How do I look?' he asked, stepping out from behind the desk.

Tyler frowned. 'Sir?'

'It's not a trick question, Constable.' Snecky gestured to himself. 'The uniform. The tie, the… How am I looking? Is the shirt OK? Not too tight? Tucked alright? Your opinion would be helpful.'

Tyler flicked his gaze up and down, then nodded. 'Aye, looking good, sir.'

Snecky tutted and dropped his arms to his sides, clearly disappointed by that answer. 'That's it, is it? I thought you lot were supposed to know all about this stuff? Style, fashion, whatever?'

'*You lot*, sir? What do you mean?'

The tiniest flicker of panic darted across Snecky's face. 'Young men,' he said. He quietly cleared his throat. 'Young men about town.'

'Oh, right. Aye. Fair enough. Thought you'd been talking to my flatmate for a minute there.'

Snecky lowered himself back into his big leather chair. 'Sorry?'

'Nothing, sir. Anyway, the reason—'

'It's for my interview,' Snecky said, cutting him short. 'The shirt's new. New tie, new epaulettes, new trousers. And then, lucky belt, lucky pants, lucky socks. Gave the shoes some spit and polish, got my sister to cut my hair, and'—he waved his hands up and down, presenting himself again—'*ta-daa.*'

Tyler smiled. He wasn't quite sure what else to do. The photo on his phone was burning a hole in his pocket, and though he was keen to broach the subject, the conversation was starting to feel like some weird dance he needed to learn the steps to before he'd be able to get anywhere.

'God, I want this job,' Snecky muttered. 'MIT. You know what that is?'

'Yes, sir.'

'Major Investigations Team,' Snecky said, explaining it anyway. 'The big boys. The A-Team. Not the actual *A-Team*, obviously. They're fictional. But MIT is where it's at. That's the goal. Murders. Kidnappings. Sexual deviants. That's what it's all about, don't you think, Constable?'

'I mean—'

Snecky leaned forward, pressing his hands together in front of his mouth like he was about to pray. 'You ever fancy yourself there, Constable? Walking the hallowed halls of MIT?'

Tyler shrugged. 'Maybe.'

'Ha!' The very thought amused the Chief Inspector. He sat back, chuckling and shaking his head. 'Well, good luck with that, is all I'll say. But me? I could be on my way there. This. Very. Day.'

He half-stood and pointed to somewhere roughly around his midsection.

'You sure this is alright?'

'It's spot-on, sir,' Tyler confirmed.

'Good. Good.' Snecky seemed genuinely relieved to hear this. He sat down again and waved a hand towards the door. 'Dismissed.'

Tyler took a half step back before remembering what he was here for.

'Um, I didn't actually tell you why I wanted to see you, sir.'

'Oh! Didn't you?' Snecky looked doubtful, like he was sure they'd already covered everything. Everything important, anyway.

'It's about this missing girl. Laura Wilder.'

Snecky didn't say anything, just raised his eyebrows a fraction. Tyler took this as permission to continue.

'She was last seen two days ago on her way to school. Nobody's seen or heard from her since. Phone's off, she's not contacted anyone, her family's really starting to get worried.'

'How old is she?' Snecky asked.

Tyler had been dreading that question. The fact it arrived so quickly in the conversation didn't bode well.

'She's sixteen, sir, but—'

'Oh. That one. Yes,' Snecky said, and what little concern there had been in his voice evaporated away. 'The repeat runaway. I saw that. We've got her as low risk.'

'Aye, but I don't think she is, sir. Low risk, I mean.'

'Oh, *you* don't think?' Snecky said. 'So, you know better than the rest of us, do you?'

'What? No, sir. That's not what—'

'You know how long I've been doing this job, Constable?'

Tyler exhaled slowly through his nose. 'No, sir,' he said, his voice falling flat.

Snecky's lips moved as he did some silent calculations, but either he couldn't work out a number, or didn't like the one he settled on.

'Quite a long time,' he said. 'I've seen thousands of cases like this, and ninety-nine-point-nine times out of a hundred, they come back when they're bored, or when they're out of money, or when they've got it out of their system.'

He sat back and interlocked his fingers over the slight curve of his belly.

'She's sixteen. She's not on any vulnerable register. She's got a history of doing a runner, turning back up, and repeat, and repeat, and repeat. This time's no different, Constable.'

'I disagree, sir,' Tyler said.

'And I don't care,' Snecky shot back. 'There's a bottle of milk in the tea room fridge that's been here longer than you have, Constable. The men and women sitting out there, collectively, have decades of experience behind them. Do you see them panicking about this girl? No. Because they, like I do, know that she'll be fine, and that we have other priorities—real priorities—to be getting on with.'

'No, I know, sir. But, she had a boyfriend. Older. She was going to break up with him. I just thought—'

'How do you know this, Constable?' Snecky demanded. 'Where are you getting this information?'

Tyler swallowed. The phone felt heavy in his pocket.

'I'm, uh, I'm friends with the family, sir. Her brother told me.'

'Aha!' Snecky cried. 'Right. I see. So this is personal, then?'

Tyler held the Chief Inspector's gaze. 'I suppose it, sir.'

'Then all the more reason for you to stay the hell away from it. We do not mix our work and personal lives here, Constable. We keep those separate.'

'I know that, sir, I just—'

'Enough!' Snecky banged a hand on the desk. The suddenness of it made Tyler jump. 'Take this as a direct order, Constable Neish. Stay in your lane. Your job, right now, is to do whatever you are told by more senior officers. And, right now, that includes everyone else in this station. If I find out you've been going rogue, and taking it upon yourself to investigate a personal matter, then I will bring the wrath of God down upon you. And Old Testament God at that, not the wishy-washy reboot.'

His chair creaked as he leaned forward, resting his elbows on the desk.

'Do I make myself clear, Constable?'

The phone in Tyler's pocket seemed to radiate heat, as if the photo was burning itself into the screen.

'Yes, sir,' he said, standing to attention. 'Crystal clear, sir.'

'Good. I'm very glad to hear that,' Snecky said. He brushed some imaginary dust off his epaulettes and straightened his tie. 'Now, in future, should you wish to talk to me, I suggest you make an appointment.'

TYLER WAS HALFWAY across the car park, speed gun in hand, when he saw him striding in the opposite direction, rubbing at his head like he was chasing away an early morning migraine.

Or a hangover, maybe.

There was a sickening feeling as Tyler's stomach dropped down to somewhere around his knees.

He shouldn't do this.

This was stupid.

This was madness.

But the phone felt so hot now, he could swear it was burning his leg.

'Um, sorry,' he began, as they passed in opposite directions. 'Detective Superintendent Hoon.'

There was a scuff of boots on tarmac as Hoon came to an abrupt halt.

Slowly, agonisingly slowly, he turned his head in Tyler's direction.

'The fuck did you just say?'

Panic prickled up Tyler's face and across his scalp. His lungs constricted until they had about fifty percent the capacity of the moment before.

'Sorry to bother you, sir. I just wanted a quick—'

'Who the fuck are you?' Hoon demanded, fully

rounding on Tyler, like he was squaring up to him in a bar fight. 'Do I know you?'

'We, um, we met yesterday, sir. At the briefing. I'm one of the new recruits,' Tyler babbled. 'You, um, you said I was a nothing person. The, uh, the offspring of a shop dummy and a sheet of A4 paper.'

Hoon's boggle eyes swivelled as they searched the younger man's face. Up close, Tyler could have sworn he smelled a suggestion of whisky on the Det Supt's breath.

'Aye, well, I was clearly bang on the money, because I have no fucking recollection of that whatsoever,' Hoon told him. 'Did I not tell you, though, that if you so much as looked at me I'd boil you alive in a vat of your own piss?'

Tyler gulped and gave a microscopic shake of his head. 'You, uh... No, sir. You didn't say that. Not... Not about the piss, sir.'

'Fuck!' Hoon barked. 'Always fucking forget that bit. What do you want?'

Tyler blinked in surprise. He hadn't been expecting to get this far. His mind raced, trying to work out the right combination of words that might get the Detective Superintendent on side.

'I, uh, I just had a disagreement with Chief Inspector Grant, sir.'

'Snecky? Aye, well, I'm no' surprised. He's a disagreeable, snivelling wee fuck. But it's none of my fucking concern, so don't waste your time coming clyping to me, son.'

He turned and began to march off. Tyler hurried after him, words tumbling out of his mouth.

'There's a girl gone missing, sir. Her name's Laura. She's my mate's wee sister. Nobody's taking it seriously, but I think something might have happened to her.'

'I'm sure it's being looked into,' Hoon said, not stopping.

'It's not, sir. She's sixteen, and she's run away before, so everyone's just sort of dismissing it, but I really think there's more to it.'

Hoon did stop at that. He spun around, sneering. 'Oh, you *really* think, do you? You don't just think, you *really* fucking think?'

Tyler stood his ground. Nodded. 'I do, sir. I found out she had an older boyfriend. Much older. She was going to break things off with him the day she went missing.'

'And how the fuck did you find that out, *Constable*?' Hoon asked, really emphasising that first syllable of Tyler's rank.

Tyler thought about lying, like he had to Snecky. But the way Hoon's eye bulged suggested he could see through anything.

'I poked around a bit, sir,' he said. 'I know I shouldn't have, and I shouldn't really be involved, since it's personal, but—'

'It's all fucking personal, son,' Hoon spat. 'All of it.'

Tyler swallowed. 'Chief Inspector Grant said—'

'Who do you trust more? Yourself, or that fucking moth-eyed scrotal growth?' Hoon demanded. 'And, be warned, if it's him, you have no fucking business being in this job.'

'Uh, no. Me, sir. I, eh, I trust me.'

'Over?'

Tyler frowned. 'Sir?'

Hoon let out a sigh that was more like a growl. 'You trust yourself *over*...?'

The penny dropped. 'Over that... moth-eyed scrotal growth, sir.'

'That's no fucking way to talk about a senior officer, son,' Hoon said. Although, for once, there was no venom in his voice. 'But I'll let it go on this occasion.'

'Thank you, sir.'

'There's your answer, then,' Hoon said.

He turned away and marched off again. Tyler really didn't want to say any more—he already felt like he'd dodged a bullet, or perhaps a full-blown nuclear explosion—but he had to ask.

'Sorry, what's my answer, sir?'

Hoon stopped.

Hoon turned.

'Ignore that prick,' he said. He looked Tyler up and down, then tutted. 'And get an identifying feature, for fuck's sake, or I'm never going to fucking remember who you are.'

CHAPTER
FIFTEEN

'HAT,' announced the barrel-chested man to the empty room at large.

He had spotted a quite remarkable-looking piece of headgear currently walking along the High Street. Well, technically the hat wasn't walking, the man wearing it was, but the hat was by far the most remarkable thing about him.

It was a grey Fedora, with a sort of flap of fabric hanging down from the back and sides, the purpose of which the man watching him on screen could only guess at. It didn't look particularly warm, so he doubted it was that.

Protection from the sun, maybe?

In December?

In Inverness?

Unlikely.

He followed him as far as the entrance to Marks & Spencer, then clicked over to check out the gaggle of

Jakeys milling about on the benches in front of McDonald's.

They were still there, still swigging from cans clutched in cold, scrawny fingers. He recognised most of them. They were largely harmless, just a bit of a pain in the arse.

He'd keep an eye.

Flicking over to the camera by the Rose Street car park, he caught a glimpse of a kid wandering on the road. A boy, three, maybe four years old, he thought, so wrapped up in jumpers and jacket that he couldn't bring his arms all the way down to his sides.

He wandered out of shot almost immediately, but a quick shunt of a lever turned the camera to follow him as he stumbled along the pavement.

'Where are you off to on your own?'

The lever was shunted again. The camera panned to reveal eight or nine other kids, similarly dressed, being marshalled along by a couple of women.

A third woman appeared behind the straggler and took his hand, and they both went skipping along to catch up with the others. A nursery group. They were headed in the direction of the Eastgate Centre. He'd clocked Santa Claus having a crafty cigarette out the back of the shopping centre earlier. Must be something on for Christmas.

The things you saw in the CCTV control room.

He switched through the cameras like he was flicking through TV channels.

A snarl-up on the Kessock Bridge roundabout.

Click.

A delivery driver arguing with a traffic warden.

Click.

An Asian couple looking up in wonder as a few flakes of snow fell out by the big Tesco.

Click.

Click.

Click.

Standard stuff for this time of day, at this time of year. It was different in the evenings, of course. People lost their minds in December, and the peak of it, Mad Friday, was just a couple of days away. The CCTV room would be fully staffed by then, half a dozen of them all watching from on high as several thousand people not used to drinking fought, and pissed, and shagged their way around the streets of Inverness City Centre.

The team would crack out the hot chocolate and the After Eights, and then bung *Now That's What I Call Christmas* on the stereo. There were few things on Earth more festive than watching a Bank of Scotland middle manager taking a shite in a wheelie bin, while Shakin' Stevens sang everyone a Merry Christmas.

He clicked back to Marks & Spencer just as the man in the hat re-emerged.

'Hat,' he said again, because it really was that noteworthy.

He wished there were someone here to share it with. The best he could do was take a screenshot and show the others later. It wasn't the same, though. There was nothing like enjoying these moments live.

There was a knock on the door. That was new. The CCTV room rarely got visitors, and when it did, they almost never bothered to knock. Generally, they just swanned in, making demands and barking orders.

'Eh, aye. In you come,' he called, nudging the joystick so he could follow the hat.

The door creaked open. A young constable he didn't recognise popped his head through the gap.

'Uh, hiya. Is this the CCTV bit?'

The barrel-chested man looked around at all the many screens and monitors.

'What gave it away?' he asked, then he beckoned the constable over. 'Here. C'mere. Check this out.'

The constable hesitated, but then sidled into the room and over to the screen.

'What do you think?' the man behind the console asked.

'Look at that hat,' the constable said. 'It's ridiculous.'

'Yes! Exactly! Thank you!'

The man grinned, clearly delighted that the new arrival shared his taste in terrible headgear.

There was a squeak as he rolled his wheelchair out from beneath the desk, then thrust out a hand that looked capable of crushing coal into diamonds.

'Dave Davidson,' he said. 'Who might you be?'

The constable took the offered hand and shook it. 'Um, Tyler. Tyler Neish. I'm new.'

'Nice to meet you, Tyler Neish,' Dave said. 'To what do I owe the pleasure?'

'I'm... I'm looking for someone,' Tyler told him.

'Is it a guy wearing the worst hat anyone's ever seen?' Dave asked. He half-turned towards the monitor. 'Because, if so...'

Tyler smiled. 'Eh, no. No. Sadly not, because I'd have struck gold there.' He reached into his trouser pocket and took out his phone.

For a moment, he just stared at the darkened screen, then he seemed to come to a decision, and pressed the button that woke it up.

Dave leaned in closer as a picture of a man and a younger girl was presented to him.

'Who's this?' Dave asked.

'Her name's Laura Wilder,' Tyler said. 'She went missing a couple of days ago.'

'Right. Sorry to hear that,' Dave said. 'Have you got a request filled out?'

'Um… a request?'

'For that morning's footage. It'll be backed up. I assume she was in the city centre, aye? About the place we cover.'

Tyler shook his head. 'No. Culloden.'

'Oof. OK. We've not got much out there. Near Raigmore, maybe. But you'll need the paperwork, and half a dozen guys to scrub through what we've got.'

'It's, eh, it's actually not her I'm trying to find,' Tyler said. He tapped the screen roughly where the man's face was. 'It's him. I want to see if we can identify him.'

Dave considered the photograph, then tilted his head back to look up at Tyler.

'Identify him? What do you mean?'

'Like…' Tyler glanced around at the monitors, chewing on his bottom lip. 'Like maybe you've seen him, or something? I know you watch people all day. Maybe you recognise him?'

Dave snorted, as if he'd just heard a good joke. When Tyler just continued to smile earnestly down at him, he realised the constable wasn't kidding.

'Oh, right. Let's see it.'

Tyler handed over the phone and waited, while Dave zoomed in on the image, tilting his head from left to right as he studied the man on screen.

'Uh-huh,' he muttered. 'Mm-hmm.'

With a nod, he handed the phone back to Tyler.

'Well?' Tyler asked.

'Vernon's Vapes.'

'What?'

'That's where he works. The new vape shop down behind Poundland. Across from where Woolies used to be.'

Tyler gawped. 'What? Bloody hell. I didn't think that would actually work. You recognise him, then?'

'No, never clapped eyes on him before in my puff,' Dave said.

Tyler's eyebrows knotted in confusion above the bridge of his nose. 'What? Then how…?'

'Left tit,' Dave said.

'Eh?'

Dave beckoned for the phone, took it back, then zoomed in and handed it back.

Tyler was no longer looking at the face he'd spent several hours studying. He was looking at a logo printed off to one side on the front of his t-shirt.

'Left tit. Vernon's Vapes.'

'Jesus Christ!' Tyler cried. 'You know how long I've been looking at that picture? I didn't notice that. I can't believe I didn't notice that. What an idiot! It was right there in front of me.'

'Aye, well, lesson learned. You'll know better next time.'

Dave wheeled himself back under the desk, and flicked one of his screens over to show a recording of the High Street earlier in the day. He hit the button to start rewinding, already grinning at the thought of what they were about to see.

'Now, check this out. Clocked it just after seven. If you thought that hat was mental, just wait until you see…'

He turned to look back at the constable, but the space where he'd been standing was empty. Dave turned to the door just in time to see it swinging closed.

'Ah well, your loss,' he muttered, then he opened his desk drawer, helped himself to a handful of popcorn, and resumed his viewing.

CHAPTER
SIXTEEN

TYLER WAS GOING to be in deep shit for this.

In fact, no. He was already in deep shit. If he got found out for this, he'd be fully submerged in the stuff.

Right now, he was supposed to be standing by the roadside of the A9, pointing the speed gun at passing cars in a bid to either encourage safer driving, or boost the country's coffers, depending on who you asked.

Instead, he was standing down an alleyway in Inverness city centre, tucked into a doorway where Woolies used to be. The flurry of morning snow had given way to icy sheets of sleet. It sliced down from the sky and splattered like thousands of tiny bomb blasts on the slush-slicked pavements.

Across the path, just a few feet from where Tyler was standing, was the entrance to Vernon's Vapes. The logo in the window was a match for the one Dave Davidson had spotted on the t-shirt in the photo.

Tyler was still kicking himself for missing that. How could he have overlooked something so obvious?

Of course, neither Mumpy nor Brian had picked up on it either, and they'd both seen the picture, too.

Then again, neither of them was a police officer.

There were three customers in the shop. Tyler could see a couple of them milling about by the racks of vapes. The other one—a blonde woman in her twenties—was at the counter, being shown how to operate her new purchase by the very man that Tyler was here to see.

The man with his arm around Laura Wilder in that photograph.

The inside of the shop was lit by harsh fluorescent strips that gave everyone's skin a sickly sheen. It wasn't a great advert for vaping.

Tyler stood, shuffling on the spot and stamping his feet to keep out the cold, waiting until all the customers had filed out of the shop. Through the window, he watched as the man from the photo unhooked a pair of headphones from around his neck, placed them over his ears, and moseyed over to straighten one of the displays.

He didn't hear the bell above the door when Tyler entered. It was only when he caught the reflection of his high-vis jacket in a window that he wheeled around, whipping the headphones off and plastering on a paper-thin smile.

'Uh, hi! Hello. How you doing?' he asked.

Tyler closed the door behind him. He could feel the sickly sweet aroma of the shop tightening his throat.

Well, it was that or the nerves.

'Aye. Not bad, thanks.' Tyler's voice sounded a touch higher than normal. Thinner. 'You Vernon?' he asked.

The man ran a hand through his thick mane of brown hair, pushing it back away from his narrow, angular face. He scraped his teeth down over his bottom lip, rasping at the strands of a straggly beard that sprouted in half-hearted patches across his chin and lower jaw.

'You what?' he asked.

Tyler pointed to the logo on the wall. 'Vernon's Vapes. Are you Vernon?'

'Oh! Right. No. There is no Vernon. It's— What do you call it? Branding. Like the Colonel for KFC, or Ronald McDonald. Or, you know, Wendy from Wendy's in America.' He shook his head, like he was admonishing himself for something. 'But less burger-based, obviously.'

Tyler opened his mouth to say something, but was cut off before he got the chance.

'I was going to get a wee mascot designed. Like, a vape with arms and legs. A face, and that. But then, I thought, what does that say? He's a vape, selling vapes.' He stared at Tyler, like he was waiting for him to appreciate the significance of this. 'Like, *he'd be a vape*, who was selling vapes. What would be the story there? Is that like, I don't know, selling people into slavery or something? Is he a pimp, and the other vapes are all prostitutes? Is that the story? I don't know. Thinking about it just totally blew my mind.'

He continued to stare expectantly at Tyler for a few more seconds, then sniffed, shrugged, and wandered behind the counter.

'Plus, it was going to cost about five hundred quid to get someone to draw it, so I knocked it on the head.'

'Right. Fair enough,' Tyler said, sidestepping almost everything the other man had just said. 'So, what's your name, then?'

'Evan.' He winced. 'Shit. I mean, what do you want to know for?'

'Evan,' Tyler said. 'Right. OK.'

He looked to the window, where people were rushing back and forth through the downpour, laden with bags of Christmas shopping. He took a moment to turn the sign on the door from *Open* to *Closed*.

'Here, what are you doing?' Evan asked. 'I'm open until one today.'

'Oh? And what are you doing after one?' Tyler asked. 'Nearly Christmas. Should you not be staying open late?'

Something in Evan's expression shifted. Tightened, maybe. His jaw clenched as he considered his answer.

'Most people aren't exactly buying vape products to put in Christmas stockings, so staying open late's a bit of overkill,' he said. 'And as for what I'm doing this afternoon, I don't see how that's any of your business.'

'What happened to your neck?' Tyler asked.

Evan ran a hand through his hair again, pulling it forward this time, trying too late to mask the mark that had already been spotted. 'Just a bruise.'

'Looks nasty. How'd you get that?'

'Just… some guy.'

Tyler raised his eyebrows. 'Some guy? What do you mean?'

'Nothing. I just… I caught some guy trying to break

into my house last night. I scared him off, but he pushed me.'

'What, he pushed you in the neck?'

Evan swallowed. 'No. I stumbled. Hit my neck on the wall.'

Tyler took a moment to try and imagine this. 'On the wall? Like, the wall of your house? Is it at an angle, or something? Is there a bit sticking out?'

'No. What? No. I don't know exactly what I bumped into.'

'You said the wall,' Tyler reminded him.

'Aye, I know, but… I don't know. The door frame, maybe. The window ledge. I don't know, it all happened quite fast.'

'You called it in, though, aye?' Tyler asked. 'An attempted break-in. You reported that, I take it?'

Evan said nothing for a few moments, then shook his head. 'Didn't see the point. He didn't stick around. I'm sure you've got plenty of other things to be getting on with.'

Tyler met the other man's eye and held it. 'We do, aye. Still, if anything like that happens again, best if you let us know.'

There was a creaking as Evan closed the hatch that cut the behind-the-counter area off from the rest of the shop. 'Will do. Now, was there something you wanted? If it's about licensing, or whatever, I've got all the paperwork, and I don't sell to anyone underage, so if someone's said I do, they're full of shit.'

Tyler took a step further into the shop, and tucked his thumbs into the pockets of his jacket. 'Funny you mention that, Evan. *Underage.* See, I'm looking for some-one. A girl. She's sixteen. Laura Wilder.'

He studied the other man's face, watching for any flicker, or any absence of one.

'You know her?'

Evan shook his head. 'Nope. Don't think so.'

'About this high,' Tyler said, holding a hand up to shoulder height. 'Blonde hair. From out Culloden way.'

'Doesn't ring a bell,' Evan said, his head still shifting from side to side.

'No? Here, maybe a photo will help,' Tyler said.

He took out his phone. He fumbled with it, and realised his hands were shaking. He forced them to stay steady as he opened up a copy of the passport picture Laura's parents had provided the police.

'That's her,' he said, turning the phone in Evan's direction.

The shopkeeper made a show of studying it. His head was still shaking. It hadn't stopped in almost thirty seconds.

'No. No, I don't think I know her.'

'You sure?' Tyler pressed. 'You sure you haven't seen her?'

'Hmm.' Evan leaned in closer and squinted. 'No,' he said, after some more thought. 'No, can't say she's familiar.'

Tyler kept the phone held out. 'Think very carefully. This is important.'

This time, Evan didn't even bother to look at the image. He just held Tyler's gaze.

'I don't know her. I haven't seen her.'

'Right. OK. Fair enough. Worth a try,' Tyler said.

He angled the phone away. Behind the counter, Evan ran a hand through his hair again, his shoulders relaxing.

'Sorry I couldn't be of more help. I hope you find her.'

'Cheers. Here's hoping,' Tyler said. 'But, actually, before I go, one more quick thing.'

He turned the phone again. Evan's gaze flitted down to it. This time, it stayed there, and Tyler enjoyed the way all the colour drained from his face.

'If you've never met her, maybe you can explain why you've got your arm around her in this photo?'

CHAPTER
SEVENTEEN

It took a long time for Evan to formulate a response. Even then, it was barely worth the effort.

'That's not me.'

Tyler laughed at that. At the absurdity of it.

'Aye, it is. It looks exactly like you. You're even wearing the same t-shirt. Look.'

He pinched on the image and zoomed in, showing a cropped shot of Evan's face and the logo on the front of his shirt.

'You seriously telling me that's not you? Have you got a twin through the back, or something? You been cloning yourself?'

Evan, having realised that this line of defence wasn't going to get him anywhere, changed tactics.

'Wait, let me… Oh, aye. Aye, that's me, right enough. Don't really know who she is, though. Just a customer, probably.'

'A customer?' Tyler said. He zoomed the image out

again. 'You always put your arms around your customers, do you?'

'I don't know, mate. I don't know who she is. I don't know what you want me to say.'

'I want you to say where she is. That's what I want.'

Evan chewed on his lip. Shook his head. His fingers tapped out an anxious rhythm on the countertop. 'I don't know anything about it. I swear.'

Tyler returned the phone to his pocket. As he did, he noticed that his hands had stopped shaking.

'See, I think you're lying. I think you do know,' he said. 'Laura had an older boyfriend. She was going to break up with him the day she disappeared.'

'No, that's... I wasn't...' Evan stammered. 'Her and her mates started coming in here two or three months back. Right after I opened. They hung out here a couple of times. That's it. Just... after hours. Drinking. Their own stuff, I mean,' he hurriedly clarified. 'They brought it themselves. I didn't give it to them or anything. Although, they said they were all eighteen, anyway, so even if I had, which I didn't...'

His voice cracked. His hands now gripped the edge of the counter. His breathing was ragged, like he was on the brink of tears.

'I swear, I... I don't know any more than that. Ask her mates if you don't believe me. I don't even have her number. I don't even know her last name.'

'I don't believe you,' Tyler told him.

'It's true, I swear to God,' Evan insisted. 'They're just some daft lassies who bought some vapes and hung out a couple of nights after we shut. I didn't do anything to anyone. I'm not like that. I wouldn't!'

The shake in his voice grew more obvious. His bottom lip trembled, like he was teetering on the edge of a full meltdown.

Before Tyler could push him over, there were two short beeps from his shoulder-mounted radio. Sharp. Urgent. Angry-sounding.

Though not as angry as the voice that followed.

'Sierra Two One, where the hell are you?'

It wasn't the calm, composed voice of someone in the Control room. It was Sergeant Hawkes.

'Tyler! You'd better bloody respond.'

Tyler winced, but otherwise didn't move a muscle. Behind the counter, Evan's gaze shifted to the radio.

'Tyler, you're supposed to be doing speed checks on the bloody A9, so what the hell do you think you're doing?'

A smile tugged at the corner of Evan's mouth. The tears that had been threatening to come now seemed like a distant memory.

'That you he's talking to?' Evan asked. 'He doesn't sound best pleased.'

Tyler breathed. In. Out. He still stood frozen to the spot, as if any movement might give his location away.

Not that it mattered. The sergeant must know where he was. Or at least know where he wasn't.

'Sounds like you might be the one in trouble, mate,' Evan said.

'You've got fifteen minutes to get back to base, Sierra Two One, or I'll be dispatching units to bring you back under lock and bloody key. Fifteen minutes, Tyler, or so help me God...'

The radio chirped into silence. The shop itself seemed to hold its breath.

Evan creaked open the hatch, and strode towards the door. With a flick, he turned the sign from 'Closed' to 'Open'. The bell *tringed* as he pulled the door wide.

'Sorry I couldn't be of more help, *Sierra Two One*. I hope you don't end up in too much trouble,' he said, flashing a smug little smirk in Tyler's direction. 'And if you find that girl, going to do me a favour?'

The smirk dropped away into a menacing sneer.

'Tell her she's barred.'

TYLER SLAMMED himself into the driver's seat of his police car, and pulled the door closed with a *bang* that rocked the whole vehicle.

'Shit. Shit. Shit, shit, shit, shit, shit!'

He thumped his hands against the wheel, then let out a primal roar so loud it drowned out the sound of a bus rushing past on the street beside him.

He'd had him on the ropes, he was sure of it. If it hadn't been for the radio, he might have got a confession out of him. He might have told him where Laura was. He might have been able to end this.

But that chance was gone. Dead. Like his police career was about to be.

He'd failed. He'd failed Laura, Mumpy, their parents.

Hell, he might as well pile on the guilt. He'd failed his

own parents, too. His tutors at Tulliallan. The other new recruits, and the old hands at the station.

Himself.

He'd failed everyone. But Laura most of all.

Tyler flexed his fingers on the wheel, and took a steadying breath. The shop was just around the corner. Maybe he could go back and question the bastard again. If he could just get something—some clue, some hint of where Laura was—then it would all be worth it. Losing his job, being dismissed in disgrace, would all be worthwhile if he could just find out where she was.

But Hawkes would've tracked the car. Tyler had realised that the moment he'd got back to it. All police vehicles had tracking installed, so that Control could see who was closest to a scene.

They'd know exactly where he was. And his fifteen minutes were already ticking down.

The turning of the key in the ignition was an admission of defeat. The engine rumbled into life, and the windscreen wipers arced left and right, swishing the slushy grey sleet off the glass.

As the windscreen cleared, a van was revealed parked a little further along the road. It was a small Volkswagen panel van, the white paint pitted with spots of rust.

Across the back doors, above an Inverness phone number, was the same logo as the one on Evan's t-shirt.

Vernon's Vapes.

'Shit,' Tyler whispered again.

He checked his watch.

'Shit!'

The sleet rattled off his jacket as he got back out of the

car and hurried over to the van. Glancing around, he checked the door handle. To his surprise, it opened, revealing nothing but a few boxes of vapes, some promotional materials wrapped in plastic, and some scattered trade catalogues.

No Laura. It had been a long shot anyway, but he had to check.

He plodded back to the car, slammed the door, fired up the engine again.

The wipers swish-swished, clearing the screen.

Revealing the van again.

This time, though, it wasn't the logo that Tyler noticed. It was the number plate.

You could get a lot from a number plate. Insurance status. MOT. Owner's name.

Registered address.

Tyler looked across to the Mobile Data Terminal mounted just below the dash. If he accessed the Police National Computer, it would flag up somewhere. Non-sanctioned usage was a sackable offence.

But then, how much more trouble could he really be in?

The wipers swished.

Tyler glanced at the number plate.

And he began to type.

CHAPTER
EIGHTEEN

THE VAN WAS REGISTERED to a residential address in Merkinch, one of the less glamorous parts of the city, and not somewhere you'd find on a postcard or a walking tour. At least, not if you wanted all your tour members to be accounted for at the end.

The route took Tyler close to Burnett Road station, which he hoped worked in his favour. If anyone was currently tracking the car, they'd see it heading in the right direction, right up until it turned off and crossed the Waterloo Bridge.

Or, as Tyler came to think of it as he powered the police cruiser up the incline towards it, "The Point of No Return."

Evan's house was just along from a Ladbrokes and a sketchy-looking pub. Hooded men stood outside both, huddling in the doorways to smoke as the sleet continued its relentless assault.

It had been almost ten years since the smoking ban in

indoor public places was introduced, but the men's body language made clear that they were all still bitter about it.

Their shadowed eyes watched him as he passed in the car, slowing to scan the numbers on the doors of the houses further up the street.

He came to a stop outside number twenty-seven. This was it. This was where Evan lived.

It was a two-storey end terrace, with an overgrown front garden, and moss sprouting all over the cracked and broken roof slates. The curtains in the upstairs were drawn, but then something about the place suggested they always were.

A narrow alleyway separated the house from the next block. Someone had graffitied the word "JIZZ" on the roughcasting of the gable end. Not in a particularly flashy way, either. There was very little artistic merit about it. Although, the scale of it—stretching several feet from J to Z—was impressive in its own way.

The front of the house was too exposed, so Tyler ducked down the alleyway, hoping there was a back gate he could sneak through. As it happened, this wasn't necessary. The tall wooden fence at the back of the house had rotted and collapsed at some point in the past.

Two panels lay higgledy-piggledy on the weed-strewn gravel, and Tyler was able to clamber over them to gain entrance to the garden.

Although, calling it a garden was misleading. A garden implied flowers, or plants, or even just a bit of grass. The rectangular space at the back of Evan's house was just gravel, six stained yellow slabs, and a cracked tarmac path connecting a gate to the back door.

And a shed. Six by four. Old, but not decrepit. A heavy padlock on the door, and a single window covered on the inside by a hanging blue tarp.

The sleet rattled on the flat shed roof, and on the brim of Tyler's cap.

'Right,' Tyler muttered, and his breath came as a cloud of condensation.

He headed for the back door of the house, and checked the handle. Locked. No real surprise. There were parts of the Highlands where you could leave your door open. Merkinch wasn't one of them. Not if you wanted any of your stuff to be there when you got back.

The downstairs windows at the back of the house were too high for Tyler to be able to look through. He stood on his tiptoes, then tried jumping, but caught only a glimpse of an untidy kitchen and a darkened living room.

There were no handy terracotta plant pots to flip upside down and stand on, or boxes on which to give himself a boost. Instead, he took out his phone, switched to the video camera, and recorded footage through both windows with his arm stretched up above his head.

He stood by the door, sheltering under the plastic canopy as he reviewed the footage. Both rooms could generously be described as looking lived in. But, right now, they could both also be described as empty.

No Laura.

No anyone.

Tyler's gaze fell on the shed. The padlock was shiny and new. Big. Sturdy. Solid.

There was another window on this side that hadn't

been visible from where he'd first entered the garden. Like its mirror image on the other wall, it had been covered on the inside.

Whatever was in there, Evan really didn't want anyone seeing it.

The back of the house was overlooked by several neighbours. There was every chance that someone would see him poking around out there, but there was no point worrying about that now. The damage was done. He was in this to the bitter end.

A check of the windows revealed no gaps in the tarpaulin curtains that would allow him to peek inside. The padlock looked brand new out of the packet, and the sort of thing more suited to protecting an industrial warehouse than a garden shed. No way he was getting through that without bolt cutters. Even then, he'd probably do himself a mischief.

Tyler returned to one of the side windows, and rapped his knuckles on the glass. It was single-paned, and rattled in the frame as he knocked.

'Hello?' he said. 'Anyone in there? Laura? This is the police.'

Nothing.

'If anyone's in there, please respond, or make a sound.'

Nothing.

Or…

Something?

He wasn't certain. He couldn't be. But for a moment, he thought he'd heard a creak. A scrape, perhaps. Some suggestion of movement inside the shed.

It could've just been the drumbeat of the sleet hitting the flat roof, or the rumbling of the wind through gaps in the planks.

But what if it wasn't?

What if Laura Wilder was right there, right on the other side of the wall, right there in that shed?

He'd need a warrant to get inside, but things changed if a life was in danger, or if a crime was in progress. If he had reason enough to believe that either of those things was true, then he *could* act. He could kick this door in. He could get inside.

And even if that weren't the case, it occurred to him again that there was only so much trouble he could be in.

His radio bleeped.

'Sierra Two One, respond. Sierra Two One, please respond as a matter of urgency.'

The voice was one of the control room operators this time, not Sergeant Hawkes.

Tyler brought his hand up to his shoulder, his thumb hovering on the button that would let him answer.

It lingered there for a moment, then moved to the power switch, and flicked it off.

'Fuck it,' he declared, then he raised his voice to a shout as he lined himself up with the door. 'Laura, stay back if you can! I'm coming in!'

He lunged, bringing a knee up to his chest, then slamming it forwards with all the force he could muster.

Pain radiated from the sole of his foot, through his ankle, up his knee, and into his hip. He stumbled, cursed, lost his balance, and thumped sideways against the door, which hadn't budged an inch.

It looked much easier in the movies.

A window. He'd break a window.

Searching the ground, he found a rock, and snatched it up. It was only as he was about to smash it against the glass that it occurred to him how light it felt.

Turning it over, he discovered a little hatch in the bottom that slid aside with a prod, revealing a shiny silver key.

'Yes. Yes!' he whispered, as the key slid into the padlock. With a twist, the lock fell open, and Tyler's hands shook as he fumbled to unfasten it from the shed's sliding latch.

Somewhere out on the street, he heard a car come to a stop. Doors opened. Closed.

Shit. *Shit*.

He got the padlock off and let it fall onto the gravel with a metallic *chink*. The wood of the door was swollen with moisture, and it took a few dunts and shoogles to get the bolt to slide free.

Footsteps clattered in the alleyway behind him.

Before him, the door sprung open a few inches.

'Constable Neish! What the hell do you think you're doing!'

It was Sergeant Hawkes. Right there, right behind him, right at his back.

Tyler pulled the door open the rest of the way, letting the grey December daylight flood in.

Boxes.

Cardboard boxes.

Stacks and stacks of cardboard boxes.

Stock for Vernon's Vapes.

'No, no, no, no,' Tyler whispered, then he yelped as a hand caught him by the arm and dragged him away from the open shed door.

There were three officers there, two older constables standing either side of their sergeant like bodyguards. Hawkes' face was a mask of fury, and knotted brow, and twisted lips, and bared teeth.

'I asked you a bloody question, Constable! What the hell do you think you're doing?' he demanded.

Tyler's mouth formed the shapes of a few syllables that he didn't quite manage to utter. What could he say? What words could he possibly come out with that would fix all this? Any of this?

He'd defied direct orders. He'd abandoned his post. He'd turned off his radio, abused the PNC database, and illegally entered a private property.

Even for him, it was a clusterfuck of epic proportions, and he hadn't even been in the job a month.

It would all have been worth it to find Laura. But he hadn't. He couldn't. Who had he been trying to kid?

'I thought she was in there,' he mumbled.

'Who?'

Tyler felt a flash of anger that he forced himself to swallow back. 'Laura Wilder. The missing girl.'

'Oh, Jesus, this again.' Hawkes pinched the bridge of his nose and sighed. 'Here's what's going to happen now. You're going to come back to the station with me, Constable, and we are going to sort this out.

'If you're lucky, you'll be fired. That's the dream scenario for you right now, because believe me when I say that there is every chance—*every chance*—that this will go further. We're talking prosecution. Jail time, maybe, if they decide to make an example of you. And, do you know what? I hate to say this, but I honestly hope they do, so that the rest of them new starts might—'

'Sarge.'

The voice came from over Tyler's shoulder. Over by the shed. It had just enough urgency to it to stop the sergeant in his tracks.

Hawkes exhaled sharply through his nose, still holding Tyler by the arm.

'What?' he barked. 'What is it?'

'You might want to take a look at this, Sergeant.'

Something about the man's tone made Tyler turn and look back over his shoulder. He pulled his arm free when he saw what the other constable was staring at.

A jacket. Dark blue, marked with spots of reddish brown.

A hammer, slick with a shine of crimson.

A rope. Some cable ties. A dirty pillowcase.

All tucked into the shadows at the corner of the shed.

'I hate to say it, Sarge,' said the older officer. 'But I think Constable Neish might've been onto something.'

CHAPTER
NINETEEN

MORE THAN ANYTHING, Tyler wanted to be back there. At the house. At the shed. At the shop, even, slapping the cuffs on Evan, and bringing the bastard in.

After the discovery in the shed, he'd been sent back to the car with one of the other constables acting as babysitter, while Hawkes had called it in.

He'd watched from behind the sleet-dappled glass as a couple of unmarked cars had pulled up. A man in his sixties had emerged from the first one, polishing off the last bite of a Tunnock's Caramel Wafer, before tossing the red and gold foil into the plastic storage pocket in the driver's door.

A woman in her thirties had joined him from the other vehicle. She looked severe, with her hair scraped back into a tight ponytail, and when she turned and shot Tyler a look, he would've sworn that she could sense every rule he'd broken in his entire life to date.

He'd inched the window down just enough to hear

her introduce them both to the constable standing guard by the car.

'DS Caitlyn McQuarrie. This is DI Ben Forde. Where's this shed?'

The constable pointed down the alleyway, and the fogging of Tyler's breath had obscured both detectives as they headed for the back garden. It was the last he saw of them.

More police cars had arrived. Half a dozen people in white paper suits had tumbled out of a minibus, as cordon tape was strung across the street.

And then, after a chirp on his radio and a few barked words from Hawkes, the other constable had climbed into the driver's seat, fired up the engine, and driven Tyler back to Burnett Road.

They had travelled in silence. It was only when they pulled up outside the station that the older officer finally spoke.

'I've to escort you inside. The Chief Inspector wants to talk to you.'

'I don't suppose he's going to offer me a promotion?' Tyler asked.

The other constable smiled thinly. 'Unlikely. From what the sarge was saying, you've royally fucked yourself here.'

Pulling on the handbrake, he'd run a hand up and down his face like he was trying to get rid of a stray hair that was tickling him.

'If it's any consolation, though, son... I get it.'

'Cheers,' Tyler said. 'Can I tell the Chief you said that?'

The constable had grinned as he opened the door.

'Can you fuck.'

Now, ten minutes after he'd entered the building, Tyler stood to attention in Chief Inspector Grant's office, as Snecky paced back and forth like a panther on the prowl.

The blinds were raised, like the Chief Inspector wanted to make a spectacle of this. The bullpen was empty at this time of day, though, so there was no one around to witness his display of power, or to share in Tyler's humiliation.

'This is unheard of,' Snecky seethed. 'This level of insubordination is… I mean, it's something else. I've been doing this job a long time, Constable Neish, and in all those years, I have never—*never*—encountered such wilful and blatant dereliction of duty. Although, let's be honest, I should've seen it coming.'

He stopped pacing long enough to snatch up a printout from his desk. The paper crackled as he flicked his wrist to straighten it.

'These are some of the comments from your trainers at Tulliallan. See what you think of these, Constable.'

He cleared his throat, glanced at Tyler to make sure he was paying attention, then started to read.

'"Headstrong." Hmm? "Easily distracted." "Overly confident." "Acts without thinking." That sound familiar? "Occasionally hysterical." I don't think it means funny there, by the way. "Prone to travel sickness."' Snecky's mouth twitched in irritation as he set the paper back down. 'I mean, that last bit's not strictly relevant, but still. It doesn't paint a great picture, does it?'

'No, sir,' Tyler was forced to concede.

'So, maybe this is my fault. What do you think, Constable? Am I to blame for all this? For you going all... all... John bloody Wayne and taking matters into your own hands? Is this somehow all my fault?'

'No, sir.'

'You're damn right!' Snecky snapped. 'That's the first true word I've heard out of your mouth since you got here. This is all on you, Constable Neish. Every bad decision, every wrong move, every line crossed, is on you, and you alone.'

'Yes, sir,' Tyler agreed. 'Have they found her, sir?'

Snecky's eyes narrowed. 'What?'

'Laura, sir. Have they found her, sir?'

'Jesus Christ.' Snecky huffed out a sigh and shook his head. 'Do you realise the trouble you're in? Whether or not the girl has been found is entirely irrelevant.'

'It isn't, sir. Not to me, sir.'

And it wasn't. The current whereabouts and circumstances of Laura Wilder were the difference between this being the worst and the best day of Tyler's life.

It was his fate that was irrelevant, not hers.

'Here's the situation as I see it, Constable. You've compromised evidence, potentially jeopardised the entire investigation. If that man walks because of your unauthorised entry, that's on you. You've accessed the PNC without authorisation. That's a criminal offence. You've ignored direct orders, abandoned your post, turned off your radio. Any single one of those is grounds for dismissal. You've done all of them in a single shift, which has to be a new bloody record.'

Snecky clenched his fists and leaned on the desk, bringing his face closer to Tyler's. 'If evidence gained from that shed is inadmissible because of how you obtained it, and this man goes free, you won't just lose your job, you'll face charges. Best case scenario, you'll never work in this job again. Worst case, you'll have plenty of opportunity to dwell on your poor decision-making from the inside of a cell.'

'I understand, sir,' Tyler said, still standing straight to attention. 'I'd just like to be kept informed on what's happening with Laura.'

Snecky's face turned red, then purple. His breathing became a throaty rasp, and the only thing that stopped him exploding with rage was the sharp, sudden knock on the door.

'Fuck me. There you are.'

Detective Superintendent Hoon hadn't waited to be invited in. He entered like a gust of wind, throwing the door so wide it clattered against a metal filing cabinet that rang out like a funeral bell.

'This you getting the fucking medal ready, is it?' Hoon asked the Chief Inspector.

Tyler staggered forward a step as the Det Supt slapped him on the back. It was like being walloped by a shovel.

'Uh, what?' Snecky asked.

'Good fucking working out there, son,' Hoon said, turning to Tyler and completely ignoring the Chief Inspector's question. 'I knew I could fucking count on you.'

Tyler had absolutely no idea what was happening, but

some tiny voice at the back of his head told him to go along with it.

'Uh, thanks, sir.'

'Sorry, what's happening?' Snecky asked, looking from Hoon to Tyler and back again.

'Constable fucking… Whoever'—Hoon jabbed a thumb in Tyler's direction—'has been doing a bit of fucking legwork for me. Well, no, donkey-work's more like it. Bottom of the barrel stuff that even this cock-brained calamityfuck couldn't make an arse of.'

He gripped Tyler by the back of the neck and shook him.

'Isn't that right, son?'

'Eh…' Tyler shot a sideways look at Snecky, then nodded. 'Aye. Aye, that's right, sir. Glad I could help.'

'Help. Fuck me. You hear that, Sammy-boy? Modest as fuck, or what? That no' make your fucking heart swell three sizes wi' pride?'

On the other side of the desk, Snecky stood gawping.

'I… suppose,' he eventually conceded, though it was clear that he had no real idea what was happening here. 'So he… Constable Neish… was acting under your authority? That really should've gone through me.'

'You're fucking right, it should,' Hoon said. He stabbed a finger at the Chief Inspector. 'That was a test, Sammy. And you fucking passed with flying colours. That's a fucking tick in the win column for your MIT application, an' no mistake.'

Snecky's face lit up at that. He smoothed down the front of his shirt, and took a moment to straighten his tie.

'Oh? Really? Well, that's… That's great.'

'Watch this fucking space,' Hoon told him. He rapped his knuckles on the top of Tyler's head, made a *knock-knock* sound, then turned back to the Chief Inspector. 'Now, I'm handing Officer Nobody here back into your care. He's your fucking responsibility now, so if he fucks up, do what you want with him. Peel off his skin and make it into a fucking hat, for all I care. I'm done with him. Alright?'

Snecky still seemed somewhat shellshocked. He nodded slowly, but his expression suggested he didn't quite know what it was he was agreeing to.

'Uh, right. Yes. I'll keep on top of him.'

'Aye, well, whatever floats your boat. What two consenting adults do in their own fucking time is none of my business,' Hoon said.

He wheeled around and was almost at the door before a blurted question from Tyler stopped him.

'Have they found her? Laura? Have they got her?'

Hoon looked back over his shoulder. 'That's above your pay grade, son,' he said. His two front teeth scraped at the greying stubble just below his bottom lip. 'But trust me, we're working on it.'

The door slammed behind him as he left the office, the force of it rattling the blinds and making the pens in Snecky's stationery pot jump around in panic.

Tyler faced front again in time to see the Chief Inspector lowering himself into his leather chair. The purple-red tinged face that had heralded an oncoming explosion had paled away into a pasty white.

Snecky picked up the sheet of paper that contained the list of Tyler's more negative qualities, scanned it, then scrunched it up and dropped it into his waste-paper basket. He looked like someone who had just lost a bet. A big one, too.

'Right. Well…' Snecky blew out his cheeks. 'I suppose, given this new information…'

'I just want to help, sir,' Tyler told him. 'I know I'm new, I know I don't really know what I'm doing, but I'll do anything you need to help find Laura.'

'You're aware she may be dead, yes?'

The words weren't cruel, just matter-of-fact.

'I don't believe that, sir,' Tyler replied. 'But, if she is, I want to help bring her family some closure.'

Snecky placed the flats of his hands on his desk and leaned back. For a long time, he said nothing, just sat there, staring up. Tyler could almost hear the whirring of the cogs behind the Chief Inspector's eyes.

'OK,' Snecky said.

He stood up and unhooked his jacket from the back of his chair.

'Sir?'

'OK, Constable. You win,' Snecky said. 'You want to help? You can come with me.'

'Yes, sir. Right, sir,' Tyler said. He watched the Chief Inspector pull on his jacket and fasten the shiny brass buttons. 'To where, sir?'

'If you're so keen to help, you can come when I break the news to the family,' Snecky told him. 'And you can explain to them how your actions might have jeopardised this entire investigation.'

CHAPTER
TWENTY

IT WAS EARLY DAYS, but so far, this was not going the way Snecky had intended.

He'd introduced himself on the front step, but Mrs Wilder had barely even seemed to notice him. Instead, she'd grasped one of Tyler's hands in both of hers and led him into the house.

Mr Wilder was in his usual armchair, but where he had once looked like a king on his throne, he now seemed to be melting into the seat, like he was too small for it, and the cushions were slowly swallowing him down.

He looked up when his wife dragged Tyler into the room, then the flicker of hope that bloomed on his face died when the solemn-faced Chief Inspector followed them in.

'What's happened?'

The question came from Mumpy. He stood by the fireplace, his bloodshot eyes and the bags hanging below them making clear how little sleep he'd had.

'Something's happened,' he said. 'What is it? What have you found?'

Tyler started to respond, but a slow clearing of the throat by Chief Inspector Grant made him take a step back.

'There has been a discovery, yes,' Snecky confirmed. He pointed from Mumpy to Mr Wilder. 'You're the brother and father, yes?'

'What kind of discovery?' Mumpy demanded.

Mrs Wilder sat on the arm of her husband's chair. It was a sudden movement, like her legs had just given way. Mr Wilder slipped his hand over hers, squeezing it.

'I'm Chief Inspector Grant,' Snecky said, as if anyone in that room gave a damn. 'Within the last hour, a discovery was made in a garden shed in Merkinch.'

Mumpy's chest rose and fell. Rose and fell. 'What *kind* of discovery?' he asked again.

'Nothing concrete as of yet,' Snecky continued. 'But there is evidence that suggests someone was held there against their will.'

'Laura?' Mrs Wilder whispered. 'Not Laura.'

'We don't know at this stage, I'm afraid.'

'Whose shed?' Mumpy asked. 'Who did this?'

'I'm not at liberty to say,' Snecky replied. He caught the look that passed between Mumpy and Tyler. 'And neither is he,' he added, as much for the constable's benefit as the family's. 'But, we have reason to believe the person who owns the shed was known to Laura.'

'Oh, God!' Mrs Wilder's hand flew to her mouth. Her fingers gripped her cheeks, the nails digging half-moons in her skin. 'Oh God, Laura.'

Mr Wilder croaked something that wasn't quite a word. It was pain given form. The hand clasping his wife's shook, as he fought back against a wave of grief that bubbled just below the surface.

Mumpy rested a hand on top of the fireplace, steadying himself. There was a photo frame there. Laura from a few years ago—the Laura that Tyler knew— grinned out from behind her prison of glass.

'Is she dead?' Mumpy asked, which drew a sob from his mum. 'Did... this guy... Did he kill her?'

'No,' Tyler said, before a stern look from Snecky shut him down.

'There's nothing at the moment to suggest that's the case,' he said. 'One of the reasons we're here is to get your assistance on something.'

This was news to Tyler. He watched as the Chief Inspector produced a glossy photograph from an inside pocket. It showed a bundle of fabric on a wooden floor, a little evidence marker tent perched beside it.

'This coat was found at the scene. We're hoping to identify it. Can you confirm this belongs to Laura?'

Mumpy snatched the photo from his hands and studied it. 'I... I think so. Mum?'

Mrs Wilder didn't take it. She couldn't. It was as if holding it in her hands would somehow make it more real. She forced herself to look at it, though, even as all her instincts tried to make her turn away.

'That's hers,' she whispered.

'You sure?' Snecky asked.

Mrs Wilder nodded. Her husband's fingers interlocked with her own. 'It's definitely hers. Or… she's got one just like it. But…'

'But what?' Tyler asked, before the Chief Inspector could stop him.

'It's an older one. I haven't seen her wearing it in a while. She said she'd lost it about a year or so back.'

'A year or so?' Tyler asked, only for Snecky to steam-roller over him again.

'But it's hers?' the Chief Inspector pressed. 'You think it's Laura's jacket?'

'I think so,' Mrs Wilder confirmed.

'Is that blood?'

It was the first Laura's father had spoken. His voice, like the rest of him, seemed smaller. Diminished.

'On the jacket,' he whispered. 'Is… Is that Laura's blood?'

'We don't know. I'm sorry. I appreciate how distressing all this must be,' Snecky said. 'We've got detectives and forensics experts at the scene now.'

'Oh, God,' Mrs Wilder whimpered. 'Oh God, oh God, oh God.'

'You've got the guy, though, right?' Mumpy asked. 'The guy with the shed. You've got him?'

'He's in custody,' Snecky said. This, too, was news to Tyler. 'Detectives from our Major Investigations Team are interviewing him now.'

'Can't Tyler do it?' Mrs Wilder asked.

Tyler blinked in surprise. Despite the seriousness of the situation, Snecky let out a snort of incredulous laughter.

'Me?' Tyler asked. He pointed to himself, just to make doubly sure he'd got the right end of the stick.

'I don't think that would be very appropriate,' the Chief Inspector said. 'The MIT is highly trained in this sort of thing, and Constable Neish is…' Snecky looked him up and down. 'Better suited to other roles.'

It was, to be fair, a more diplomatic answer than Tyler had been bracing himself for.

'But Tyler knows her,' Mumpy said. 'Tyler was actually looking for her, when everyone else just palmed us off.'

'They didn't know, son,' Mr Wilder said.

'Bullshit. I don't care!' Mumpy cried. 'Tyler looked. Tyler actually bothered his arse.'

'I understand that you're upset—' Snecky began, but it was his turn to be cut short.

'Upset? I'm not upset, I'm fucking raging!' Mumpy hissed. 'Who found it? The shed? Who found the jacket, and whatever else it is you've got?'

Snecky clenched his jaw. 'That was Constable Neish,' he conceded. 'But the manner in which he made the discovery means—'

'I knew it. See? Because he cares! He gives a shit!'

'Mumpy, mate…' Tyler said, raising a hand to calm him. 'It's alright. We're on this. It's going to be alright.'

'This is why Tyler should be in there questioning that man,' Mrs Wilder insisted. 'He was always so good to Laura, and she always liked him. Always, since she was tiny. She always loved you, son.'

Tyler felt his eyes start to sting. He wasn't going to

cry, though. He wasn't going to let them see that, and worry about what it meant.

'Aye, I heard!' he said, summoning a smile from somewhere. 'I heard she had a right crush on me!'

Mrs Wilder laughed. Despite herself, despite everything, she laughed. It was like a pressure venting just in the nick of time.

'A crush? On you? No, she thought you were...' Mrs Wilder caught herself in the nick of time. 'She thought of you like a big brother.'

'Oh. Right. Aye!' Tyler said. 'Course.'

He thought of those girls at the school.

Are you her brother's mate?

The one she fancied?

The one she had a crush on since she was eight?

'Can we get him put on the case?' Mr Wilder asked. 'Tyler, can we get him made... I don't know, deputy detective, or however it works?'

Snecky did a decent job of hiding his amusement. Had Tyler not been looking for it, he might not even have noticed.

'I'm afraid that's not possible. And it wouldn't be in Laura's best interests. Constable Neish doesn't have the necessary skills or experience to help bring Laura home.'

'And yet, it's all because of him that you're actually taking it seriously,' Mumpy said. 'So maybe skills and experience aren't what we need right now.'

Snecky smiled thinly. 'Yes. Well. We'll have to agree to disagree on that one, I'm afraid. Rest assured, we are doing everything we can to bring your daughter and sister back home, and to hold accountable anyone who might have harmed her in any way. May I?'

He held out his hand for the photograph. Mumpy didn't look at it as he passed it back.

'I'll get a trained liaison officer assigned. They'll be round as soon as they can, and will be able to answer any questions you may have, as well as providing updates as and when we have them,' Snecky said, sliding the photo back into his pocket. 'As I said, please rest assured that we are doing everything possible.'

'We are, mate,' Tyler said, meeting Mumpy's eye. 'Seriously, we're on it. We've got the bastard. They'll get him to talk. Whatever he's done with her, he'll tell us.'

Mumpy mouth moved, like he was chewing back a sob. His jaw tensed as he looked down at his parents holding onto one another on the chair.

'Cheers, Ty,' he said, and his voice became a broken whisper. 'I really hope you're right.'

'YOU HAVE REALLY LEARNED nothing from all this, have you?' Snecky barked as he accelerated his SUV away from the Wilders' house.

'Sir?'

The Chief Inspector shot Tyler a sneering sideways look.

'You shouldn't have opened your mouth in there. Promising them the world like that.'

'I didn't promise them anything!'

'Maybe not in so many words, but you set a certain expectation. You've given them hope.'

Tyler frowned. 'And? Why's that bad?'

'Because how are they going to feel if their daughter turns up in the river? Or in pieces? Are they going to thank you for that hope?'

'I think they'd have more on their mind at that point, sir,' Tyler replied. 'I don't see what harm it can do in the meantime.'

Snecky muttered something uncomplimentary below his breath, and tightened his grip on the wheel.

'Right, from tomorrow, you're on Bosco Maximuke duty.'

Tyler stared out at the road ahead. The big tyres of the SUV were making short work of all the many potholes, but the way the vehicle rolled on its axis was doing his stomach no favours.

'What does that involve, sir?'

'Standing, mostly. Standing in the rain. I hear it's going to be pissing down and blowing a hoolie. And you'll be standing outside one of Bosco Maximuke's building sites, watching it all day long.'

'OK,' Tyler said. Then, after a moment, 'Wait, why?'

'Because I said so, Constable. I know following direct orders is new to you, but deviate one iota from this one, and you are done. Hoon or no Hoon. You are finished.'

'Eh, right. Aye, sir. No worries. But, I mean, how will I know what I'm looking for?'

Snecky hung a big right around a roundabout. Tyler's stomach sloshed around like it was trying to make its escape.

'You'll be looking for anything. Any flicker of movement. It's four days until Christmas. Any legitimate building yards are all shut down. Bosco Maximuke is suspected of being one of the biggest importers of narcotics into this country. If there's activity at his yards, you can rest assured it won't be because they're building someone a conservatory.'

'They're not all shut, though,' Tyler said. 'Are they? Not all builders, I mean.'

'Well, Constable Neish,' Snecky said, pressing the accelerator to the floor. Tyler swallowed back a mouthful of hot, sour saliva. 'That'll be what you're standing there in the pouring rain to work out.'

CHAPTER
TWENTY-ONE

TYLER CLOSED HIS LOCKER, turned the key, and then ran a hand through his hair, trying to tease some life back into it. He could already tell it was a lost cause.

Besides, his heart wasn't in it. Somewhere in the building, Evan from Vernon's Vapes was being interrogated. He hoped Detective Superintendent Hoon was the one doing the questioning. Evan had almost cracked under pressure when Tyler had been talking to him. If Hoon let rip, he was likely to completely implode.

Tyler finished lacing up his trainers, pulled on his jacket, and headed for the door. He left the locker room with every intention of going straight home, so was slightly surprised when his feet started to plod him in an entirely different direction.

There was something bothering him. Something that he couldn't quite put a finger on. Something that had been said at the house, or in the car. There was something somewhere that didn't make sense, and he could feel it wriggling around in his brain, refusing to be pinned down.

He let his feet lead the way. They walked him past offices and storage cupboards, past interview rooms and tea rooms, and quiet spaces where families came to grieve.

It was only when he arrived at a big swing door, that he realised they'd been retracing his steps from earlier that day.

When he spotted Constable Dave Davidson through the door's little porthole window, the brain worm stopped wriggling. Not fully. Not all the way. Just enough for him to see the edges of it, and to understand its shape.

He knew why he was here. He knew what had bothered him. Not one thing that had been said, but two.

The building yards. The building yards were all shut.

The other thing was still just a theory. Less than that, in fact. A feeling in his gut, nothing more.

Taking out his phone, Tyler rattled off a text to Mumpy. It was about Laura, about what she'd thought of him. How she'd seen him.

Are you her brother's mate?

The one she fancied?

The one she had a crush on since she was eight?

'Twice in one day!' Dave Davidson said, when Tyler slid into the room. 'You here to check out that hat again?'

Tyler smiled and sidled up to Dave's desk. There were a couple of other people in shirts and ties sitting at other stations now. One was a young woman with a hearing aid who was munching her way through a bag of Malte-sers. The other was a man in his sixties who sat poised and unmoving in front of his screen like a gargoyle.

'Eh, no. Not the hat,' he said. 'I was, um, I was hoping you could help me look into something.'

Dave lowered his voice to a whisper. 'What, like a top-secret mission?'

Tyler stole a look at the other two operators in the CCTV room. 'Aye, something like that,' he confirmed.

Dave sat back in his wheelchair. 'Nah, no can do,' he said. 'Sorry.'

Tyler started to protest. 'It's just… I just need…'

'I mean, if you just want to look at something on here, no bother,' Dave told him. 'But I can't be arsed doing any James Bond shit at this time of day. It's nearly knocking-off time.'

It took a moment for Tyler to understand what he was hearing. 'Oh! Right! You can… You can show me something?'

'Depends on where and when.'

'City centre. Last night,' Tyler said.

Dave sucked in his bottom lip, then spat it out again. 'That,' he said, before pausing for dramatic effect, 'is not a problem.'

He turned his attention to his controls. Tyler's phone buzzed in his pocket, as Mumpy's reply arrived.

No, Mum was right, mate. She didn't think of you like that at all. It wasn't you that she had the crush on.

. . .

TYLER'S THUMBS tapped at the screen as he wrote a response, then sent it off into the electronic ether.

By the time he'd finished, Dave was gesturing to a screen on his left. It was split into four images, all showing different parts of the city centre.

'High Street area. Last night. Got a rough time?'

'Not really,' Tyler conceded.

'Right, then you might pull up a chair,' Dave said, rolling himself back a little. He indicated the controls. 'Forward, back, pause. Click that to go full screen. Zoom with that, but it's shite, so I wouldn't bother.'

'Shit, shit! There!'

Tyler pointed to the top right image on the screen. It showed the entrance to an old church on Bank Lane that was now a nightclub. It had been a few nightclubs over the years, and would likely continue to evolve, given the rate at which previous owners had collapsed into bankruptcy.

By the time Dave looked up, there was nobody in the frame but a couple of bouncers.

'What, them guys?' he asked.

'No, go back. Go back a bit,' Tyler urged. 'Just a few seconds.'

His phone buzzed in his hand. He didn't look at it. Not yet.

Dave tapped a button, and all four images spooled backwards. A drunken man on the bottom left staggered backwards. A bent-double woman inhaled vomit off the pavement, before straightening up again.

And on the top right, three figures Moonwalked out through the nightclub door.

Dave hit pause without having to be told. With a tap on his console, the image grew to fill the screen.

Three men stood there. Big, burly, *proper men*. Working men. Tyler had only met them the once, but they weren't exactly easy to forget.

Edgar. Big Gary. Moobs.

A boys' night out.

Tyler looked down at his phone. His heart thumped against the inside of his chest, because he knew. He already knew what was going to be written there.

He saw his own previous message first. The question he'd sent.

IF IT WASN'T *me she had the crush on, who was it?*

AND THEN, below that, Mumpy's reply.

A single word.

A single name that changed everything.

BRIAN.

'HE'S NOT THERE,' Tyler realised. 'He's not with them. He didn't go on the night out.'

'Who?' Dave asked.

'And the yards are shut. It's nearly Christmas. Builders' yards aren't open.'

Dave still wasn't following. 'So?'

Tyler looked down at his phone. At the name of his flatmate.

'So where the hell has he been going the last few days?'

CHAPTER
TWENTY-TWO

'BRIAN?'

Tyler stood in the hallway of the flat, listening for any sound from behind Brian's bedroom door. He'd checked in the other rooms, but found them empty. The kettle was warm to the touch, suggesting it had been used within the last hour or so, but there was nothing else to indicate anyone was home.

'You there, Brian?' Tyler asked. He gave a knock on the door, quietly at first, like he was worried about disturbing anyone inside, and then louder when he got no response.

The hinges creaked as the door opened. Tyler had heard the sound a thousand times before, but it seemed louder now. Deafening. A telltale heart in the silence.

Brian's room was a mess, though no more than usual. His work clothes lay strewn across an old IKEA padded chair. Irn Bru and Coke cans were stacked on the floor and the bedside table, like he'd left while in the middle of building a defensive perimeter around the unmade bed.

The air was so thick with the smell of cannabis that Tyler would've sworn it clung to his skin, and clogged up his pores. An overflowing ashtray sat on the chipped and battered bedside table, an open wooden box beside it revealing roaches, and Rizlas, and a half-finished roll-up.

Tyler sniffed at the ashtray. It was hard to be sure, but the smoke smelled recent, like Brian had only recently stubbed out his last dog end.

He wondered, just briefly, if he should phone this in. Tell Sergeant Hawkes, or Snecky. Hoon, even.

But what would he say? That his flatmate hadn't gone out on his work night out, after all? That he'd been the subject of Laura's childhood crush, not Tyler? That he'd been leaving the house every morning, and coming back every evening, like he usually did?

Hardly a smoking gun.

And yet, though he wished more than anything to be wrong, Tyler's gut told him he was onto something.

So, if he couldn't call it in, there was nothing else for it.

He grabbed a pillow, gave it a shake, then tossed it aside. Same with the other one.

The mattress was heavy, but he hoisted it up onto its side and let it fall against the wall, revealing the mess beneath Brian's bed. Work boots, and battered trainers. Condoms, and tissues, and half-empty Durex gels.

Stray socks, charger cables, magazines, and old glass bongs.

Nothing that told him anything, though. Nothing that helped.

He tore through the drawers in the bedside table, ripping them out and tipping their contents onto the floor. Junk. All junk. Nothing useful. Nothing that told him anything at all.

By the time he'd finished, the room looked like a tornado had torn through it. Posters had been pulled down, furniture had been upended, and the wall of cans lay scattered across the carpet.

And Tyler was no further forward. There was nothing here that connected Brian and Laura.

But, of course there wasn't. Tyler lived here, too. If Brian was involved with Laura in some way, this was the last place he'd bring her. He wasn't an idiot.

Far from it.

He'd been leaving every morning.

He'd said he was going to work.

The building company. The yard. If Snecky was right, they were all closed until January. The perfect place to stash someone.

Or to hide a body.

Fortunately, Tyler had dropped Brian off half a dozen times in the past, when he'd been too hungover to drive himself.

He knew where the yard was.

He just didn't know what he'd find when he got there.

❇

THE RAIN WAS a baptism across his face. It was also fucking freezing, but he was too heavily invested now to care.

The tall metal fence wobbled unsteadily as Tyler clambered over it, the wind whistling its outrage around him as he struggled to hold on.

The drop to the other side was seven feet into a puddle of dark, dirty water. He landed with a splash that soaked his jeans, and ruined a perfectly good pair of trainers.

Ahead of him, several Portakabins lurked in the depths of the evening gloom. Cement mixers, and piles of lumber, and miniature diggers had been covered by tarps that rattled and flapped as if desperate to get away from there, to make their escape.

He'd parked around the corner and snuck up on foot, eyes peeled for Brian's car. There was no sign of it parked along the street out front, though, and the only vehicles in the yard itself were company-branded vans and flatbed trucks.

He wasn't here. Was that good? Tyler no longer knew. Rational thought had been driven out by the pure instinct that had made him climb the fence without any idea what he might be getting himself into.

If he was lucky, maybe it would return. Until then, instinct was all he had.

The icy rain hammered at him, as if trying to drive him back as he scuttled, head down, to the closest hut. A light above the door blinked into life as he approached, dazzling him and drawing a hiss of shock through his teeth.

Shit, shit!

He ran, keeping low, until he was pressed into the shadows at the side of the Portakabin. Tyler waited, breath held, until the security light turned itself off again.

Raising his head, he peeked in through the window. The cabin was set out like an open-plan office, with piles of receipts on spikes and blueprints pinned to the walls.

With the torch of his phone, he could see all the way from one end of the space to the other. Empty. No Brian. No Laura. No anyone.

That left two more Portakabins. Both looked identical to this one from the outside. Along with this one, they formed three sides of a square, surrounding the parked vans.

If you reversed right up to the door, you'd be able to drag someone inside without anyone from outside the yard seeing you.

But with all these vehicles parked there, that would be impossible. You'd have to pull up behind them, forty feet or more from the nearest door. That was a long way to lead a struggling hostage, or to carry the dead weight of a body.

Risky. And Brian wasn't an idiot.

Far from it.

Tyler's gaze shifted to the gap between the nearest two cabins. There, tucked away near the back wall of the yard, was a metal storage container with enough space out front to park a double-decker bus.

Sticking to the wall so as not to activate the security light, Tyler made his way around the side of the cabin and picked his way across the uneven ground. The surface of the yard was a quagmire of slippery, wet mud that almost cost him his balance three or four times.

Eventually, he stumbled upon a long, narrow indent that compressed the mud down, making it easier to walk on. A tyre track that led all the way to the shipping container.

Thunder rumbled somewhere far off in the distance. The rain doubled down, as if responding to a direct command. It tore at Tyler's skin, soaking him, slicking him, blinding him as he approached the metal door.

There was no point listening. There could be an orchestra playing in there, and he wouldn't hear it over the howling of the storm.

His hands were numb, painfully numb, as he grabbed the top slide bolt and wrenched it down, then pulled the bottom one from its mooring in the poured concrete base.

The heavy door groaned mournfully as the wind inched it open. This time, Tyler didn't bother with a deep breath, or an encouraging mantra, or any sort of preparation whatsoever.

Instinct drove him on.

Instinct opened the door.

Instinct shone his torch into the cold, clammy darkness.

Even over the rattling of the rain, he heard the sob that rose from deep down in his throat.

The oval of light picked out a chair, plastic and metal.

Picked out a girl, beaten and bloodied.

Picked out the shine in her eyes, and the tears on her cheeks, and the tremble as she braced herself for what was to come.

'Laura?' he whispered. 'Laura, it's me! It's alright. It's me, it's Tyler!'

Her eyes widened in the darkness. A noise got trapped beneath the rag that was tied across her mouth.

Tyler didn't have time to register the splash of a puddle behind him before pain exploded across the side of his head.

The world turned itself off and back on again, rebooting just as he went sprawling sideways into the mud, his phone flying from his hand before it and its light sunk out of sight.

'Oh, shit!' a voice hissed from the freshly cut darkness.

Tyler tried to get up, but his legs weren't having it. Not yet. Not quite.

The world swam into focus just in time to see the outline of a figure standing above him, a spade in his hands.

'Jesus Christ, mate.' Brian groaned, his fingers tightening on the spade's wooden handle. 'I *really* wish you hadn't come here.'

CHAPTER
TWENTY-THREE

'Brian. Stop.'

Tyler's raised hand was shaking. There was blood on his fingers. A ringing in his ears. His voice sounded faraway, like it was someone else speaking on his behalf.

'I told you to leave it,' Brian seethed. The ambient light from the city picked out the lines on his face. He looked pained by this. By what he'd done. 'I fucking told you she'd be fine!'

'She's not fine,' Tyler wheezed. Mud oozed between his fingers as he slid himself backwards, eyes locked on the spade in Brian's hands. 'Look at her. Look at what you did to her.'

'We were working it out!' Brian cried. 'We were. She just… I needed to talk to her, that was all. I needed time to make her see sense. She was going to tell everyone, Ty. About us, me and her.'

'You and her?'

An older boyfriend.

She'd been going to break things off.

'She fucking threatened me. Can you believe that?' Brian asked. He seemed outraged by the thought, and tightened his grip further on the shaft of the spade. 'Daft wee lassie like her, threatening *me*? Saying she'll tell everyone I'm a fucking paedo!'

He glared into the shipping container, nostrils flaring like a bull about to charge.

'Brian. Look at me,' Tyler said. 'Down here, look at me.'

It took a few seconds, but Brian's gaze eventually flicked back to Tyler.

'Did I make mistakes? Aye. I'll own up to that,' he said. 'I shouldn't have done it. Any of it. But she came onto me, not the other way round. She was up for it. She fucking loved it!'

Tyler slid back until his head was resting against the container's metal wall. 'How long?' he asked. His voice sounded closer now, but still not quite his own. 'How long have you been seeing her?'

Brian tensed. Sniffed. Shrugged his shoulders. 'I don't know.'

'Listen, Bri, if I'm going to help you, mate, I need to know. I need to know everything.'

'Help me? What do you mean? You're not going to help me.' Brian's face twisted into a sneer. 'Why the fuck would you help me?'

'How long?' Tyler asked.

The jacket in the shed had gone missing a year ago. Nine months before Vernon's Vapes had opened its doors. Nine months before Laura had ever set eyes on Evan.

'I don't know.'

'How long, Brian?' Tyler roared the question, like he was trying to outdo the rumbling thunder.

'Two years. Three. I don't know,' Brian spat back.

Jesus.

Oh, God.

Fourteen? Thirteen? Was that how old she'd been?

'You see?' Brian muttered. His face was wet. Rain, mostly, but not only that. 'You see why I couldn't let her say anything? It'd be the end of me, mate. What would the boys say? What about my mum? My wee mum. What would she think of me, if she knew?'

His voice cracked. He stamped his feet and whipped his head from left to right, like he could shake off his sorrow, and his shame. Anger rushed in to take their place.

'She did this. She made me do this,' he said. 'She's fucking ruined everything.'

'We can sort this, Brian,' Tyler told him. He braced his feet against the wet ground, digging his heels in as deep as he could. 'Just… give us a hand up, mate, and let's talk about it. Alright?'

Brian rubbed at his forehead, gritting his teeth as the icy rain hammered down like some divine judgement from on high.

'I'd love that, Ty. I'd love it if we could do that,' he said, his voice barely audible above the ever-worsening weather.

His hand returned to the handle of the spade. His fingers flexed, then wrapped around it.

'But you're lying. I know you're lying. See, you've always been a bad liar. It doesn't suit you. You're too honest, too much of a fucking goody-goody. And I fucking love you for that, Ty. I do, so it breaks my heart that you're here. It does. But, I can't have everyone finding out. I can't have people knowing. Not the boys, not my mum, not any—'

The handful of mud hit him square in the face, the stone wrapped inside it striking the bridge of his nose with a sharp, sickening *clunk*.

Sprackling in the mud, Tyler scrambled to his feet and dived before Brian could bring the spade up. His shoulder slammed into his flatmate's midsection, and all the air left his body in a puff of misty white air.

They went down together, all arms, and legs, and blood, and spit. A flailing fist caught Tyler on the side of the head. He ignored it. Hissed through it, grabbing for Brian's arms, trying to pin him down, hold him back, restrain him.

Brian twisted beneath him. A knee powered into Tyler's ribcage, and pain exploded up his side and across his back. He cried out, then gagged as a fistful of mud was shoved into his open mouth.

Still, he held on, choking, blinded, bleeding. The ground was a swamp beneath them, dragging them down, pulling them in.

Brian's head came up suddenly. Tyler barely managed to twist his face away before the headbutt struck the top of his eye socket.

Ignore it. Fight through it. Carry on.

Blood poured into his right eye and fell onto the twisted mask of rage that was Brian's face.

The world, already dark, dimmed further around the edges. Tyler's arms became lead.

Still, he held on.

If he stopped, if he lost, if he failed, then it was over. For him, for Laura. They were done for.

And there was no way he was letting that happen.

'Stop. Fucking. Fighting me!' Tyler bellowed.

He got a thumb into the pressure point where Brian's left hand met the wrist. Brian howled with pain as Tyler pressed, and twisted, and forced the arm down.

Yes. Yes!

He could do this. He *was* doing this!

The second headbutt came out of nowhere. This time, the world flashed white, like all the security lights in the yard had turned on at the same time.

When the darkness returned, Tyler lay on his front, coughing and choking on blood and wet dirt. Footsteps squelched through the mud beside him.

He saw the spade, just a few feet away. Saw Brian stumbling towards it.

And he lunged, slipping, scrabbling across the wet ground, grabbing for the weapon before Brian could reach it.

His fingers found the handle and tightened around it. He spun as best as he could, swinging awkwardly. The spade connected, though not seriously. Not hard.

Brian, already off-balance, staggered just enough to give Tyler an opening. Feet sliding out from under him, he dragged himself upright, raising the spade, readying to swing.

'Don't!'

The warning came from inside the shipping container. Tyler's eyes had adjusted just enough to the gloom to be able to make out the shape of Brian standing directly behind Laura's chair.

Thunder rumbled, and lightning flashed, reflecting off the girl's wide, terrified eyes. And off the blade of the Stanley knife held to her throat.

'Stay where you are. I'll slit her fucking throat.'

'Don't do this, Brian,' Tyler said. The words popped on his lips as bubbles of bloodied spit. 'It's over. Give it up.'

'It's not over!' Brian cried. 'I know what I'm doing! I've got a plan!'

'Evan? The guy from the vape shop?' Tyler wiped the blood from his lips, but more soon took its place. 'You saw the logo, didn't you? In that photo. I didn't notice it, but you did.'

Brian said nothing. The raw, animal sound of his breathing echoed around the inside of the container.

'How did you find his house, though? I can't work that bit out.'

Silence.

Then, 'Companies House website.'

'Jesus,' Tyler whispered. 'Of course. Limited company. Director's address. Easy, really.'

The world was starting to undulate back and forth. Concussion, maybe. Tyler hadn't been on the inside of one before, but he imagined this must be how it felt.

He let the metal head of the spade fall to the ground, and leaned on it for support.

'They know, by the way,' he said. 'That Evan didn't do it. It was the jacket. She lost that ages ago. Left it with you, I'm guessing.'

'In my car,' Brian said, without prompting.

'In your car,' Tyler mumbled. 'Right. Of course. Well, they know it wasn't Evan.'

'It doesn't matter,' Brian hissed. 'They don't know it was me.'

'Oh, come on, mate. Seriously?' Tyler said. He tried to chuckle, but there was too much blood and filth in his throat to let him. 'You said it yourself, I'm no Sherlock Holmes. You think I figured all this out myself? I've got half of Burnett Road Police Station on its way here right now.'

Brian hesitated.

'You're lying.'

'Listen. Come out here. You can hear the sirens,' Tyler said.

Brian didn't move. Behind her gag, Laura whimpered as the blade remained pressed against the front of her neck.

'You're talking shit. I don't believe you!'

'It's over, Brian,' Tyler insisted. 'Give it up before you go too far. Laura's alive. I'm alive. We're all alive. Nothing is fucked beyond all recognition here. We can make the best of this.'

'The best of what?' Brian sobbed from the darkness. 'I already told you, I can't have people knowing. You know what they do in prison to people they think are paedos? I can't go to jail. I can't do all that to my mum!'

'Think about her, Bri. Your mum. Wee Maggie. Think what she'd say if she was here. She'd tell you to put down the knife and come out. Wouldn't she?'

'Shut up! Don't talk about her. Don't say her name!'

'She wouldn't want her son becoming a killer. What would that do to her, mate? How would she come back from that?'

'I can't. I can't go to jail.' Brian was babbling now, the knife trembling in his hand. 'I don't want her looking at me. I don't want her looking at me, knowing what I've done.'

'She's your mum, Brian. I know her. She'll love you, no matter what.'

'No. How? How could she? After this. After what I've done. What I am.'

'Put down the knife, Brian. Come out. Let Laura go.'

'I can't. I can't. I can't!'

His voice became a cry, became a shout, became a scream.

The blade moved suddenly in the darkness. Tyler heard the swish of metal through flesh. Heard the gagging, and choking, and the gasping for air.

Tossing aside the spade, he ran. Another flash of lightning tore across the sky, revealing the blood on Laura's face.

And on the walls.

But mostly on the chest and throat of Brian as he dropped to his knees, warm crimson spraying from the neat line that ran from one side of his throat to the other.

'No, no, no. Brian. Brian!'

Tyler slid to his knees beside him. The knife slipped from Brian's bloody fingers and rattled against the floor. He fell backwards, still on his knees, his body bending like his legs were made of foam rubber.

His eyes were wild and wide as he gulped and garbled, his hands still by his sides, making no attempt to stifle the blood flow.

There was so much of it. So much red. The warmth of it pumped between Tyler's fingers as he tried his best to apply pressure, to stem the torrent, to turn back the tide.

Brian stared. Bubbles formed in the blood beneath Tyler's hands.

And in the darkness of the suddenly silent shipping container, Constable Tyler Neish became a proper copper, and finally earned his place.

CHAPTER
TWENTY-FOUR

'JESUS FUCK, son. I know I said to get a distinguishing feature, but I meant a funny walk, or a wee moustache. "Face fucked by the Michelin Man" is a bit of an extreme fucking look to go for.'

Tyler raised a hand to acknowledge Detective Superintendent Hoon's arrival at the back door of the ambulance. The paramedics had checked him over to make sure he wasn't about to drop dead, but only after they'd checked Laura. He'd stood firm on that.

Or, technically, he'd sat firm, his legs pretty much refusing to hold him upright by then.

The other ambulance had already left, bringing Laura to the hospital. The fact it hadn't cranked on the flashing lights or the sirens was a good sign, he hoped.

He'd managed to get the gag out of her mouth, but the world had started spinning from the effort, and when it became a choice between trying to cut her free and calling for help, he'd opted for the latter.

She had screamed for a while. A long time, in fact. He'd lain there on the floor, in the slowly expanding puddle of blood, doing his best to keep her calm as sirens wailed far off in the distance.

Her parents had been called. Mumpy, too. They were already on the way to the hospital to meet her. Sergeant Hawkes had told Tyler that news himself, right between calling him a daft bastard and a liability.

Both were fair, Tyler thought. He couldn't really argue with either.

'What the fuck happened to you?' Hoon asked.

'Nothing good, sir,' Tyler croaked.

'Aye, you can fucking say that again,' Hoon said. 'So, what are you fucking lying there smiling for?'

'Am I, sir?' Tyler asked. He shrugged. It hurt. He didn't care. 'I hadn't noticed.'

There was a scuff of footsteps on tarmac. Hoon stepped aside, and the older man Tyler had spotted back at Evan's house appeared by the ambulance's open back door. Ben something. A DI.

He chewed quickly on something, pointed to his mouth to indicate he'd just be a moment, then forced it all down with a painful-looking swallow.

'Sorry, didn't have lunch. Or dinner, for that matter.' He looked to Hoon, but tilted his head in Tyler's direction. 'This him?'

'That's him,' Hoon said.

'He looks rough.' Ben said.

'Aye, well, he's been clanged in the napper with a big fucking spade, by all accounts. You ask me, the Quasimodo look does fucking wonders for him.

Finally gives the beige nonentity a bit of fucking character.'

'Rough around the edges, I meant,' Ben said.

Hoon snorted and crossed his arms. 'I mean, that goes without fucking saying. He's like a child in a man's body. And an idiot child at that. In fact, you know who he reminds me of?'

'No. Who?'

'What's that fucking film?' Hoon asked. 'With them two rapists. Are they rapists?'

'I don't know. I don't know what film you're talking about,' the DI told him.

Hoon tutted. 'For fuck's sake, Benjamin. The film. The fucking... with the mental wee lad. He's constantly fucking torturing them.'

'Who, the rapists?'

'Aye, the rapists! Or maybe they're not rapists. Why would there be a pair of rapists in a fucking kids' film?'

'There wouldn't be,' Ben reasoned.

'Well, no' these fucking days, anyway. The way we fucking mollycoddle the grasping wee bastards,' Hoon muttered. 'Anyway, the wee lad. Awful wee arsehole. He's torturing them. Setting them on fire, fucking... I don't know. Nailing them to the wall, pouring bleach in their eyes, pissing on them, or whatever.'

'Jesus,' Ben muttered. 'You sure this is a kids' film?'

'Aye! Come on. It's a Christmas one. It's a fucking classic. That smug wee prick's in it! I can fucking picture him now. On the cover. He's doing this.'

Detective Superintendent Robert Hoon of the Police Scotland Northern Major Investigations Team slapped both hands to his cheeks, opened his eyes wide, and pulled a face like he was screaming in terror.

'Home Alone,' Tyler volunteered from the back of the ambulance.

'Yes! Fuck me! Thank you!' Hoon cried, stabbing a finger in Tyler's direction. 'Home fucking Alone. Does he no' look like that entitled wee sack of shite from that?'

Ben considered this, tilting his head left to right as he studied Tyler's face. 'Not really,' he finally concluded.

'Fuck. No. Maybe you're right,' Hoon admitted. 'Oh, well. Anyway…'

He leaned into the ambulance, caught hold of one of Tyler's sodden trainers, and gave the foot a shake. It hurt immensely, but Tyler was far too exhausted to react.

'Good fucking work out there, Mr Nobody. Your face might be hanging in tatters, and it'll probably haunt my fucking dreams for the rest of my life, but that lassie's alive because of you.'

'Cheers, sir.'

'I mean, your mate's dead, obviously, but you can't win 'em all, eh?'

'Uh, no. No, I suppose not,' Tyler agreed.

Hoon clapped his hands and rubbed them together, then turned back in the direction of the building site. Police car lights flickered across him, painting his face in alternating shades of red and blue.

'Right, where the fuck's Geoff Palmer? I've no' had a chance to have a go at him for shiteing himself on that bus.'

Practically salivating at the thought of the piss-taking he was about to deliver, the Detective Superintendent marched off into the rain. Tyler watched him until a sudden flash of movement in the air beside him caught his eye.

Something landed on the blanket beside him. The red and gold wrapper seemed to glint in the light.

It was a biscuit. A Tunnock's Caramel Wafer.

'Good work out there, son,' Ben told him. He shoved his hands in his pockets and rocked back on his heels. 'I'll be keeping an eye on you.'

With a nod, he too vanished out of sight.

Only to reappear again a moment later. He looked deliberately at the biscuit on the bed at Tyler's side.

'You are going to eat that, aye?'

Tyler looked down at the Caramel Wafer again. 'Um, aye, sir. Yeah. Definitely.'

'Right.' Ben looked a little disappointed, but managed to put a brave face on it. 'Well, make sure you do. And, you know, don't get used to it. Those things don't grow on bloody trees.'

And with that, he was gone. Properly, this time.

Tyler felt his phone buzz in his pocket. He rummaged around under the blanket until he was able to wrestle the mobile free from his pocket.

There was a text message on the screen. It was from Mumpy.

THANK YOU.

. . .

TYLER'S ARMS were too heavy for him to reply, his thumbs too stiff, his eyes too swollen. He would deal with it later. He had a lot he had to deal with.

He wanted to check in on old Mr Franklin and Sandra. Maybe bring them a wee something for Christmas. Nothing big, just a token gesture.

That lad, too. Callum. The scratches on his arm and the way he'd spoken about his dad had started alarm bells ringing that Tyler was only now really hearing for the first time.

He'd swing by there, too. Follow-up. That was allowed. That, he could justify.

And from there, who knew? A new flat, probably. A difficult conversation with Brian's mum. An apology to Evan at Vernon's Vapes might not go amiss, either.

So much to do. But he had time.

He was a proper copper now. He'd earned his place.

In more ways than one.

As the back doors of the ambulance closed and the engine rumbled to life beneath him, Constable Tyler Neish unwrapped his Caramel Wafer, and took a bite.

And then almost choked to death on the bloody thing, as he surrendered to the welcoming arms of sleep.

JOIN THE JD KIRK VIP CLUB

Want access to an exclusive image gallery showing locations from the books? Join the free JD Kirk VIP Club today, and as well as the photo gallery you'll get regular emails containing free short stories, members-only video content, and all the latest news about the world of DCI Jack Logan.

JDKirk.com/VIP

(Did I mention that it's free…?)

GET MORE FROM JD KIRK

Read more of JD Kirk's writing, free of charge, on his Substack.

hackofalltrades.substack.com

GO BACK TO THE BEGINNING

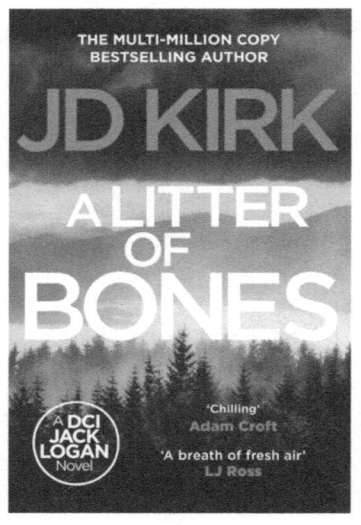

Follow Tyler's career progression in the DCI Logan series.
Read on for the first chapter of book one, A LITTER OF
BONES.

A LITTER OF BONES

CHAPTER ONE

THE TOTAL COLLAPSE of Duncan Reid's life began with a gate in the arse-end of nowhere.

There was a trick to opening this particular gate, Duncan knew. The arm of the metal slider had been buckled for years, and if you tried hauling it in the direction the bend suggested it should go you were doomed to failure. The trick was to twist and jiggle, creaking the slider loose of its mooring, allowing the whole thing to eventually swing free.

Or, if you were a seven-year-old with more energy than sense, you could clamber up the metal spars, jump down, and stand triumphantly on the other side waiting for your dad to get a move on.

"I win," cheered Connor. He broke into a little dance. *The Floss*, he called it. All the rage, apparently.

Down at Duncan's feet, their Golden Retriever wriggled impatiently, the entirety of her copper-coloured backend wagging, her front feet pawing at the ground with barely contained excitement.

"Alright, Meg. Give us a minute," Duncan told the animal.

The slider *clunked* free. The gate had barely swung six inches towards him when Meg nosed it open and squeezed through. Connor dodged aside as the dog went haring past him. She bulleted ahead, running for no other reason than the sheer unbridled joy of being out of the car and off the lead.

"Someone's in a hurry," Duncan remarked.

They watched as she detoured off into the trees that lined the track on the right, quickly vanishing from sight beneath the moss-covered trunks.

"Meg!" Connor called after her. "Come back."

"She'll be fine," Duncan said. He pulled the gate closed behind them, wiggling the slider just enough to jam it shut, but not so far that he'd have to go through the whole process again when they left. "She's been exploring round here since before you were born."

Connor didn't look convinced but fell into step beside his dad as they set off along the track.

Living up here, they were spoiled for choice when it came to dog-walking routes. Granted, it was pretty much the only thing they were spoiled for choice for, but it was something. But, of all the routes available to them, this one stood out as a favourite.

The only downside was getting to it. The drive along the main Fort William to Spean Bridge road could be a nightmare in the summer. At this time of year, though, before the campervans piloted by overly cautious tourists had started to clog everything up, it flew by.

After that, it was just a turn up the Leanachan Forest road, a mile or so along a single-track lane with the fingers crossed that no-one was coming the other way, and then the usual wrestling match with the gate.

And then… bliss. Miles of forestry track, cracking views, and rarely another living soul in sight. In all the years that Duncan had been making the same walk, he'd met maybe twenty walkers, half a dozen cyclists, and one guy on stilts.

That one had caught him off guard and had sent Meg into a frenzy of panicked barking. It was a sponsored hike for charity, it turned out. Cancer, or something. Duncan had been too busy trying to get ahold of the dog and quieten her down to really pay too much attention.

Once he'd got her by the collar, he'd chucked a couple of quid into the collection tin and kept hold of Meg until the guy had teetered off around the corner, out of sight.

Today was looking like it'd be free of interruptions, and Duncan felt physically lighter as he let himself relax. Meg was a good dog, for the most part, but didn't handle strangers well, so the lack of life signs always came as a relief.

Sure, someone might come around one of the bends further down the track and set her off, but that was a problem for later. For now, the coast was clear.

Far off on the left, across a graveyard of tree stumps, the A82 curved ahead to the Commando Memorial, and onwards to Inverness. An irregular stream of traffic meandered up it, paintwork glinting in the uncharacteristically bright April sunshine.

At this distance, the traffic was whisper quiet. The only sounds to be heard were the *chirping* of the birds, and the faint crunch of the stony ground beneath Duncan's boots.

Up ahead, Meg exploded from within a crop of trees, ploughed through a mud puddle that painted her brown from halfway down her legs, then stopped in the middle of the path. She watched them for a while, tongue hanging out and chest heaving as she checked that they were still headed in the same direction.

When she was sure they weren't about to turn around and head for the car, she returned to the trees, getting back to whatever business she'd left unattended in there.

"See, told you she'd be fine," Duncan said, giving his son a playful nudge. "Filthy, I'll give you, but fine."

"Did you see how much mud is on her?"

"I did."

"She's *covered*!"

"She is. And guess who's cleaning her up when we get home," Duncan said.

Connor grinned up at him. "You!"

"Me? No way! You!" Duncan said.

"Nuh-uh!"

"Yuh-huh! I'll give you a scrubbing brush and a bucket," Duncan said. He gave a little gasp as an idea hit him. "You can do the car when you're at it. Two birds with one stone."

Connor shook his head emphatically.

"Fine. You can hold her while I hose her down."

Connor had no real objection to that, but it had become a game now, and so he continued to resist.

"Nope!"

Duncan stroked his chin, his finger and thumb rasping against his stubble. "OK, she can hold you, and I'll hose *you* down." He made a sound like skooshing water, and mimed blasting the boy with it. "How about that?"

Connor giggled. "I had a bath this morning."

"You did? God, is it April already?" Duncan teased.

Connor didn't quite get the dig but giggled again, regardless.

They walked on for several minutes, rounding the gentle curve of the track, passing the little quarry on the left-hand side, where two diggers had sat mostly motionless for the past year or so. Rarely, when Duncan came up this way, they'd have moved a few feet, or the angle of the buckets would have shifted. He'd never seen any sign of anyone sat behind the controls, though, much less doing any actual digging.

It had been a while since Connor had said anything, and although Duncan was enjoying the peace and quiet, it wasn't normal. Friday was swimming day at school, and the boy would normally be full of stories about who was proving to be the best at backstroke, and which of his classmates had come closest to drowning.

Today, though, he'd barely spoken a word that Duncan hadn't teased out of him first.

"You alright, Con?"

"Yeah, fine," Connor said, not looking up. He had

found a stick that was almost the height of himself, and was walking with it like a wizard with a staff.

"If Meg sees you with that, she'll be away with it," Duncan warned.

Connor nodded, but said nothing.

"How was swimming?"

"Good."

"Everyone survive?"

Connor nodded. "Yep."

They continued on in silence for a while longer. A bird of prey circled in the air above them. A buzzard, Duncan guessed, although he had no idea. It might've been an eagle. It could've been a big pigeon. He'd lived his life in the Highlands, but the particulars of its wildlife were lost on him.

Similarly, the trees lining the tracks beside them. He had no idea what those were, either. Pine? Maybe. Beech? Very possibly. Oak? He didn't think so, but he had no idea what he was basing that on. They were trees. That was about as specific as he could get.

"Dad?" Connor said, after a few more steps. His eyes were still fixed on the ground, his voice quiet. "You know Ed?"

Duncan ran through his mental checklist of the kids in Connor's class. He couldn't place an Ed.

"Which one is he? The one with the orange mum?"

Connor glanced up at him, brow furrowed in confusion. "Next door Ed."

"Oh, *next door* Ed. Yes. Sorry. I thought you meant someone in your class."

"There's no-one in my class called Ed," Connor replied.

"No, I know. I was…" Duncan gave his head a little shake. "Next door Ed. Aye. What about him?"

Connor seemed to wrestle briefly with his next question. "Do you like him?"

Duncan puffed out his cheeks. "Do I like him? Next door Ed?" He shrugged. "Suppose. I mean, I don't really know him. He seems nice enough. I think he's settling in alright. Why?"

Connor tapped the ground with the bottom of his stick as they walked, drumming out a little beat.

"Does Mum like him?"

Duncan stopped. "I don't know. Why, what makes you ask that?"

Connor walked on a few paces, then he stopped, too. He stood there, chewing his lip, twisting the staff in his hand. "Nothing. I was just wondering."

Duncan cocked his head a little, regarding his son quizzically. "That's a weird thing to just start wondering."

Connor's cheeks blushed red.

"Con?"

"Where's Meg?" the boy suddenly asked, his eyes darting to the tree line.

"She's in there. She'll be fine," Duncan said, shooting the forest the most fleeting of glances. "She'll come back when we call her. Why were you asking about—?"

"Meg!" Connor shouted. "Meg, where are you?"

He put his fingers in his mouth and attempted a whistle. All he managed was a blast of damp-sounding air.

Duncan sighed, then formed a C-shape with thumb and forefinger and jammed them in his mouth. His whistle was shrill and loud. It cut off the birdsong, instantly reducing it to an indignant sort of silence.

"Where is she?" Connor asked, scanning the trees. "Why isn't she coming back?"

"She'll be fine," Duncan assured him, but he gave another whistle and followed with a shout. "Meg! Come on, Meg!"

Nothing moved in the trees. The canopy of leaves and branches cast the undergrowth into a gloomy darkness. There was still an hour or so until sunset, but the shadows were growing longer, and the breeze had gained a chillier edge.

"Stupid bloody dog," Duncan muttered.

"What if she's hurt?" Connor fretted. "What if something's happened to her?"

"Nothing will have happened to her. She's probably just rolling in something. You know what she's like."

Duncan cupped his hands around his mouth and called the dog's name again.

"Me-eg!" he shouted, stretching it across two syllables.

They waited. The trees creaked. The wind whispered through the grass.

But beyond that, nothing.

"Bugger it," Duncan muttered.

"Dad?" said Connor, his eyes wide with alarm. "Why's she not coming?"

"She'll be fine. She's always fine," Duncan said. "But I'll go in and look for her, if it makes you feel better. You stay here and shout me when she comes back."

Connor glanced both ways along the empty track, then nodded. "But what if she doesn't?"

"She'll be back," Duncan promised.

"But what if she's not?"

"She will."

"But—"

"I won't stop looking. Alright?" said Duncan, a little irritably. He forced a smile. "She'll be fine. She's just being a pain. You wait here."

Connor nodded again. "OK. I'll wait here."

"Good lad. And shout when she comes out. Nice and loud, alright?"

"I will, Dad."

Duncan clapped a hand on the boy's shoulder. "And don't worry. We'll get her. She won't have gone far."

"Bastard," Duncan hissed, clutching his cheek where a thin branch had whipped at him. There was no blood, but he could feel a welt forming, raising a thin red line across his skin.

The ground was moist and spongy beneath his feet, and a dampness crept up the legs of his jeans, sticking them, cold and clammy, to the tops of his ankles.

"Any sign, Con?" he called over his shoulder.

"Not yet!" his son shouted back, his voice muffled by the surrounding woodland.

Duncan cursed the dog a few times, then just cursed

in general as he trudged onwards, his boots snagging in the undergrowth, the branches determined to have one of his eyes out.

Half a dozen shambling steps later, something moved suddenly on his right, rustling through the tangle of grasses. He turned, startled, almost losing his balance as he searched for the source of the sound.

A rabbit appeared briefly from a knot of weeds, realised its mistake, then vanished again just as quickly. Duncan didn't see it again, but heard it scamper off to some hiding place deeper into the forest.

"Bloody thing," he grumbled, listening to the fading *swish* of the rabbit through the grass.

He was only a couple of minutes' walk into the trees, but light was already in short supply. Everything was painted in a gloominess that turned the shadows to pools of black and tinted everything else in shades of grey and blue.

"You got her, Connor?" Duncan shouted.

He waited for a response from his son.

"Connor?" he called again, when no answer came. "You got Meg yet?"

Nothing.

"Con?"

The trees groaned around him. The breeze murmured through the undergrowth. Everything else had fallen silent.

Looking back, Duncan wouldn't be able to say for sure why he ran. Not really. There was nothing to suggest anything had happened. No one thing he could pinpoint as the reason for his sudden panic. Realistically, Connor simply hadn't heard him. That was all. It wasn't unusual for the boy to get distracted. His selective deafness was an ongoing family joke.

And yet, Duncan ran. He ran, fuelled by fear, pushing his way through the grasping undergrowth and the whipping branches, splashing through the soggy dips, and stumbling over the moss-covered rocks, something hot and urgent gnawing away at his insides.

"Connor!"

He hurtled out of the trees, slipped on an unexpected embankment, and slid down it on his arse. The puddle of mud at the bottom cushioned his fall, then *schlopped* forlornly as it lost its grip on him when he pulled himself free.

"Con? Connor?"

He'd emerged from the forest thirty feet or so from where he'd first entered it. He had a clear view of the spot where he'd told Connor to wait, but hurried over to it, anyway, in case he was somehow overlooking something.

In case he was somehow overlooking his son.

Where the boy had been was a long, crooked stick, lying on the ground. A staff, abandoned by its wizard.

"Connor?" Duncan bellowed. His voice echoed in both directions along the empty track, up into the forest, off across the graveyard of stumps, and on towards the distant road. "Connor! Where are you? Con?"

And then, from behind him, came the sound of movement.

He sobbed, relief flooding him, lightening his head, slackening muscles he hadn't felt go tight.

"Connor, I thought I told you to—?"

He stopped when a muddy Golden Retriever padded out of the trees, tail wagging, tongue lolling happily.

Something deep in Duncan's gut twisted into a knot. He spiralled around, searching for his son. "Connor!" he bellowed. "Con, where are you?"

No answer came. Meg crept to Duncan's side, her head low, sensing his distress.

"This is your fault! Stupid bloody dog!" Duncan snapped.

Meg lowered her head, her eyes gazing uncomprehendingly up at him.

Duncan's voice softened. It took on a pleading edge. "Go find him. Go find Connor," he said. His fingers fumbled for the phone in his pocket as he stared at the dog, willing her to listen, willing her to understand.

He thumbed the phone awake. No signal. *No fucking signal.*

Duncan shot the dog a desperate, hopeless look. His voice cracked.

"Go find our boy."

Made in United States
Cleveland, OH
17 January 2026

31171162R00111